BEN 10 X

OMNIVERSE ™ MC

1

GHOST SHIP

STORY BY
CORY LEVINE

ART BY
ALAN BROWN

BEN 10: OMNIVERSE
VOLUME 1
GHOST SHIP

STORY BY CORY LEVINE
ART BY ALAN BROWN

DESIGN/SAM ELZWAY
EDITOR/JOEL ENOS

BEN 10 CREATED BY MAN OF ACTION

PRINTED IN CHINA

PUBLISHED BY VIZ MEDIA, LLC
P.O. BOX 77010
SAN FRANCISCO, CA 94107

10 9 8 7 6 5 4 3 2 1
FIRST PRINTING, OCTOBER 2013

vizkids
www.vizkids.com

www.viz.com

GHOST SHIP
VOLUME 1

TABLE OF CONTENTS

THE OMNIVERSE —————————————— 4

GHOST SHIP

CHAPTER 1: FOWL FIGHT ———————— 6

CHAPTER 2: THE GHOST SHIP ————— 20

CHAPTER 3: DOWN THE HATCH ———— 30

CHAPTER 4: SHOCK TO THE SYSTEM — 47

BONUS SKETCH ——————————— 62

THE OMNIVERSE

WHEN HE WAS TEN YEARS OLD, BEN TENNYSON DISCOVERED THE OMNITRIX, A DEVICE THAT SAVES AND CATALOGS DNA AND CAN TURN ITS WEARER INTO DIFFERENT ALIEN FORMS, COMPLETE WITH THE POWERS OF THE ORIGINAL ALIEN. BY TURNING INTO DIFFERENT ALIENS IN TIMES OF NEED, BEN BECAME A SUPERHERO, BATTLING THE FORCES OF EVIL FOR THE NEXT SIX YEARS. NOW LIVING IN A HIDDEN ALIEN COMMUNITY ON EARTH, UNDERTOWN, SIXTEEN-YEAR-OLD BEN IS SADDLED WITH A NEW PARTNER, ROOK, A BY-THE-BOOK MEMBER OF AN ELITE TEAM OF SPACE COPS KNOWN AS "PLUMBERS." AND NOW BEN IS BEING HUNTED BY A NEW ENEMY, A BOUNTY HUNTER CALLED KHYBER WHO HAS A FIERCE PET DOG WITH HIS OWN VERSION OF THE OMNITRIX, ALLOWING IT TO TURN INTO THE NATURAL ENEMY OF ANY ALIEN BEN CAN TURN INTO!

BEN TENNYSON
AGE 11
WHEN HE WAS 11 YEARS OLD, BEN WAS JUST LEARNING HOW TO USE THE POWERS OF THE OMNITRIX TO BATTLE THE EVILS OF THE UNIVERSE.

BEN TENNYSON
AGE 16
NOW BEN IS A SOLO SUPERHERO, OR AT LEAST HE WANTS TO BE. LIVING IN UNDERTOWN, HE'S WORKING WITH A STICK-IN-THE-MUD NEWBIE PLUMBER PARTNER, ROOK.

ROOK BLONKO
ROOK JUST GRADUATED FROM THE ACADEMY AND KNOWS ALL THE RULES BUT HAS NONE OF BEN'S EXPERIENCE. PLUS, HE'S KIND OF CONFUSED BY EARTHLINGS AND THEIR WEIRD WAYS... ESPECIALLY BEN'S.

MAX TENNYSON
BEN'S GRANDPA MAX IS A RETIRED PLUMBER HIMSELF WHO HAS TAKEN IT UPON HIMSELF TO TRAIN BEN AND HIS COUSIN GWEN IN THE WAYS OF SAVING THE UNIVERSE. IT'S HIS IDEA THAT BEN AND ROOK WORK TOGETHER SO EACH CAN LEARN FROM THE OTHER.

KHYBER
AN ALIEN BOUNTY HUNTER WHO HAS BEEN WATCHING BEN FOR YEARS AND HAS FINALLY DECIDED THAT DEFEATING THE 16-YEAR-OLD HERO WILL BE HIS CROWNING ACHIEVEMENT.

KHYBER'S PET
KHYBER'S FEROCIOUS ALIEN DOG WEARS A NEMETRIX, WHICH CARRIES THE DNA OF EVERY PREDATOR THAT WOULD EVER STALK ONE OF BEN'S ALIENS. HE'S THEREFORE THE ULTIMATE FOE TO BEN 10!

LIAM
HE MAY LOOK LIKE A BIG CHICKEN, BUT HE'S REALLY MORE LIKE A BIG BULLY... WHO LOOKS AND ACTS LIKE A CHICKEN. NOT THE MOST FUN COMBO.

BEN 10 OMNIVERSE

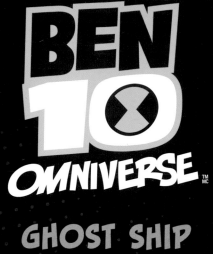

GHOST SHIP

CHAPTER 1
FOWL FIGHT

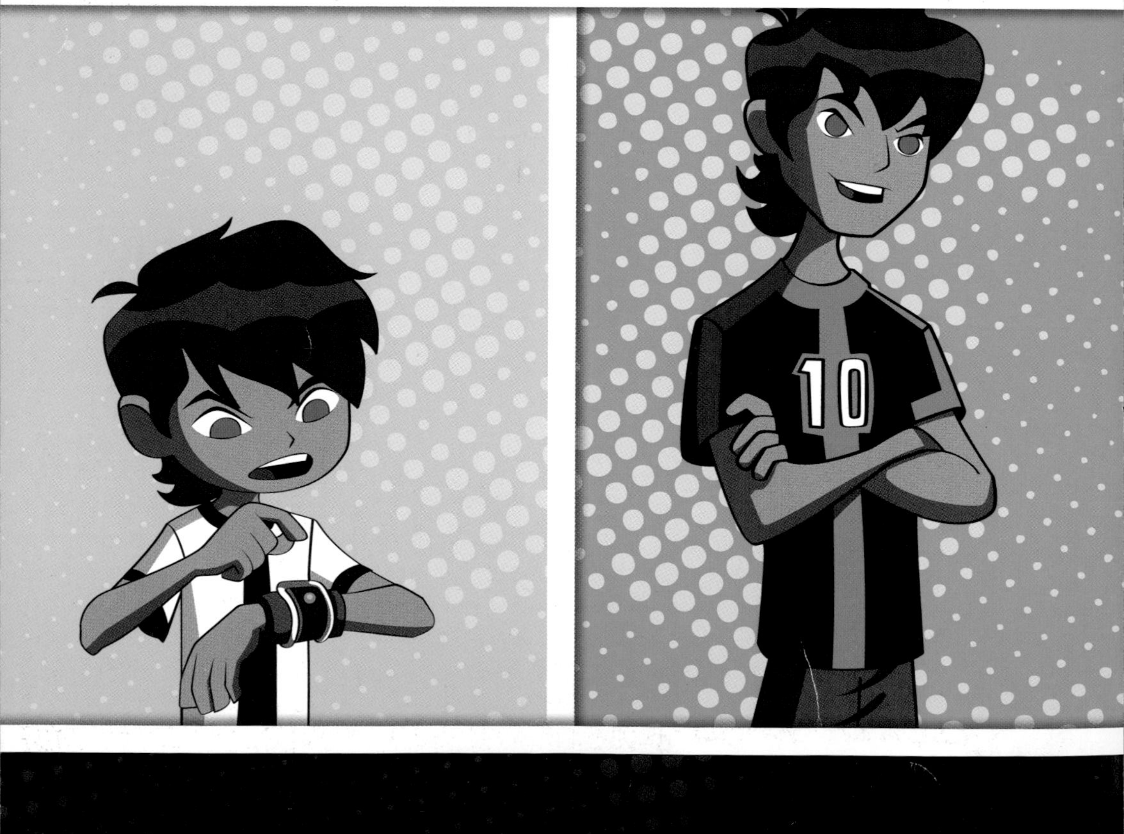

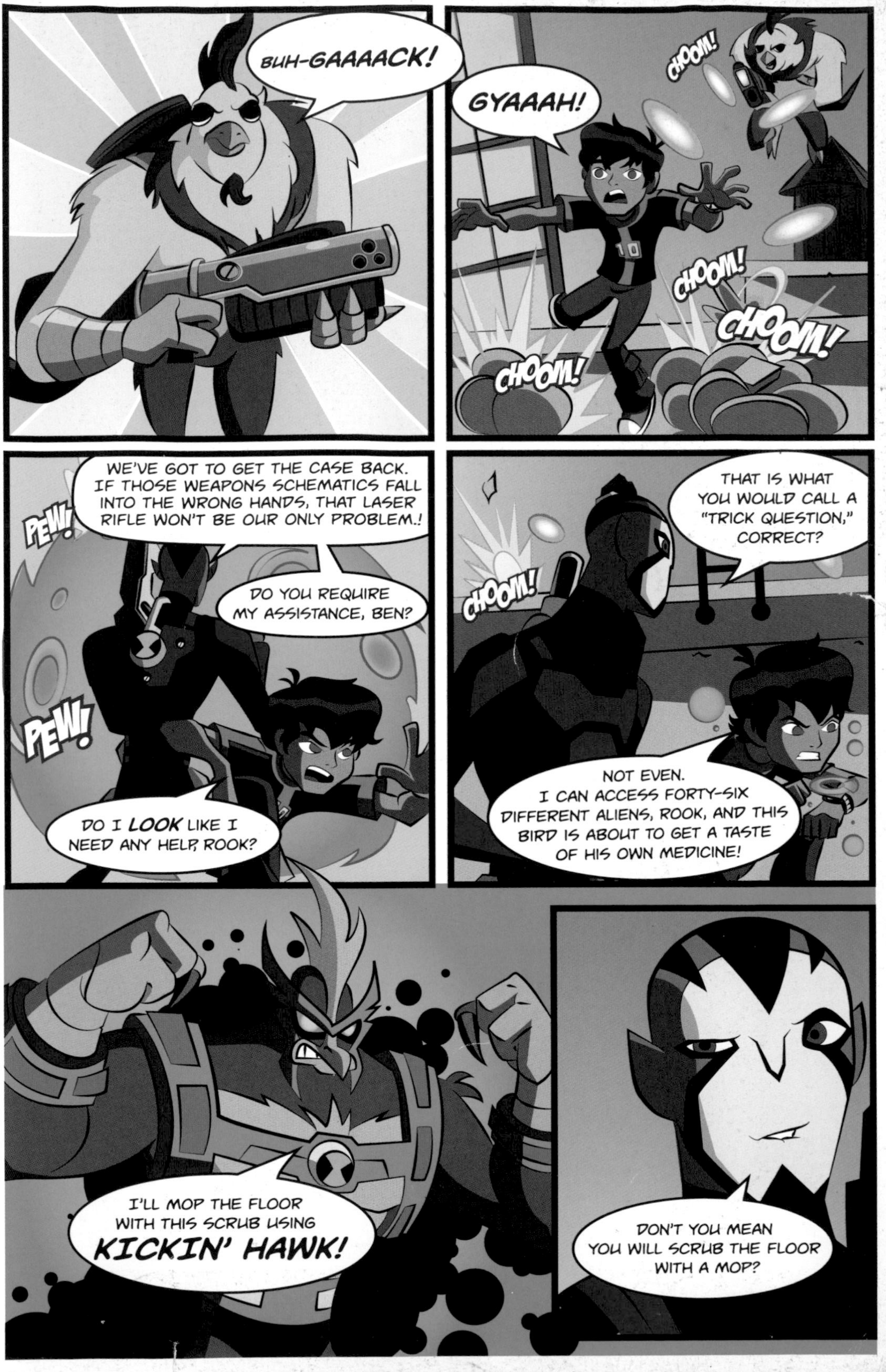
BUH-GAAAACK!
GYAAAH!
CHOOM!
CHOOM!
CHOOM!
CHOOM!
WE'VE GOT TO GET THE CASE BACK. IF THOSE WEAPONS SCHEMATICS FALL INTO THE WRONG HANDS, THAT LASER RIFLE WON'T BE OUR ONLY PROBLEM.!
PEW!
DO YOU REQUIRE MY ASSISTANCE, BEN?
PEW!
DO I LOOK LIKE I NEED ANY HELP, ROOK?
CHOOM!
THAT IS WHAT YOU WOULD CALL A "TRICK QUESTION," CORRECT?
NOT EVEN. I CAN ACCESS FORTY-SIX DIFFERENT ALIENS, ROOK, AND THIS BIRD IS ABOUT TO GET A TASTE OF HIS OWN MEDICINE!
I'LL MOP THE FLOOR WITH THIS SCRUB USING KICKIN' HAWK!
DON'T YOU MEAN YOU WILL SCRUB THE FLOOR WITH A MOP?

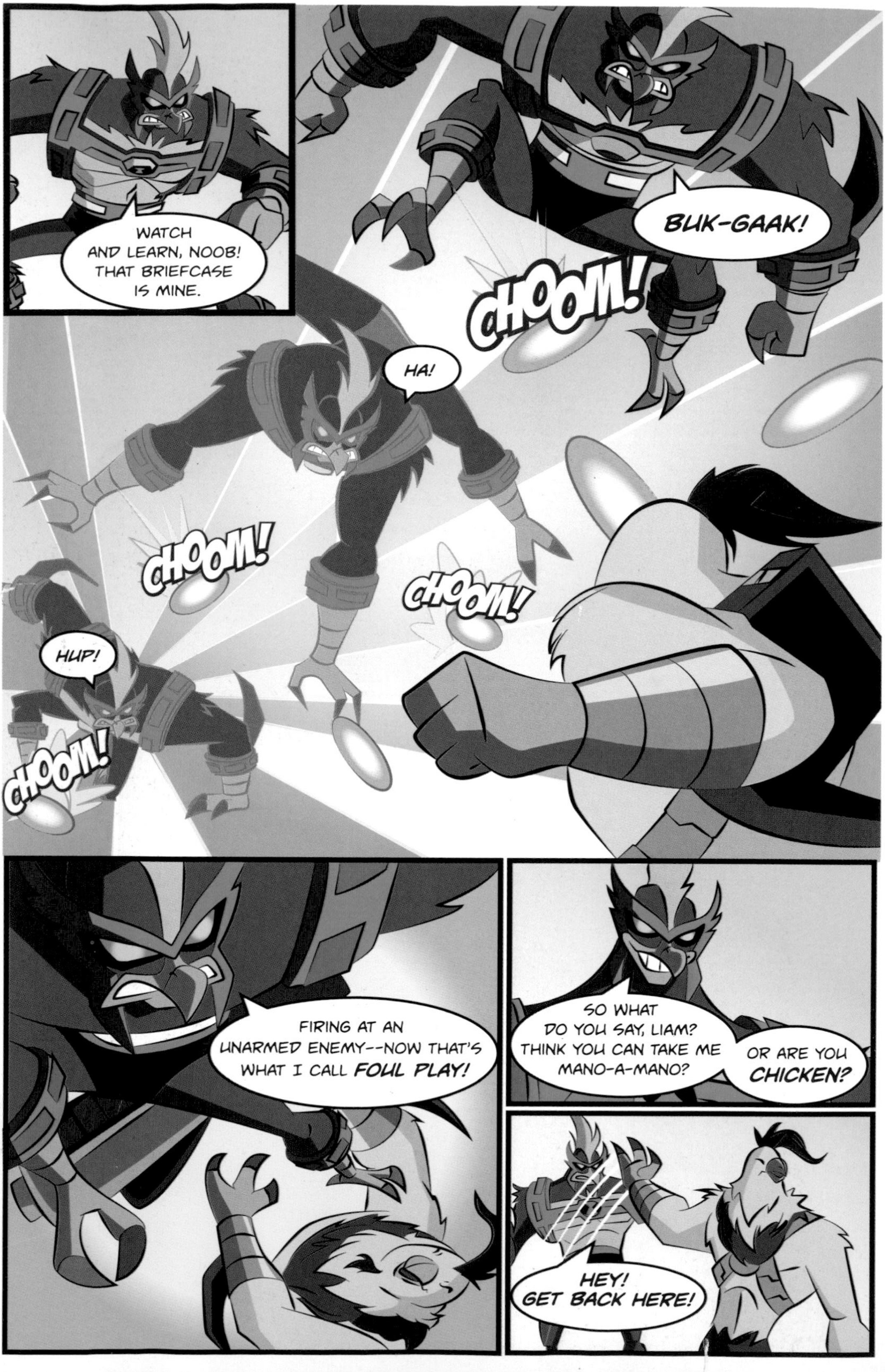
WATCH AND LEARN, NOOB! THAT BRIEFCASE IS MINE.
BUK-GAAK!
CHOOM!
HA!
CHOOM!
CHOOM!
HUP!
CHOOM!
FIRING AT AN UNARMED ENEMY--NOW THAT'S WHAT I CALL FOUL PLAY!
SO WHAT DO YOU SAY, LIAM? THINK YOU CAN TAKE ME MANO-A-MANO?
OR ARE YOU CHICKEN?
HEY! GET BACK HERE!

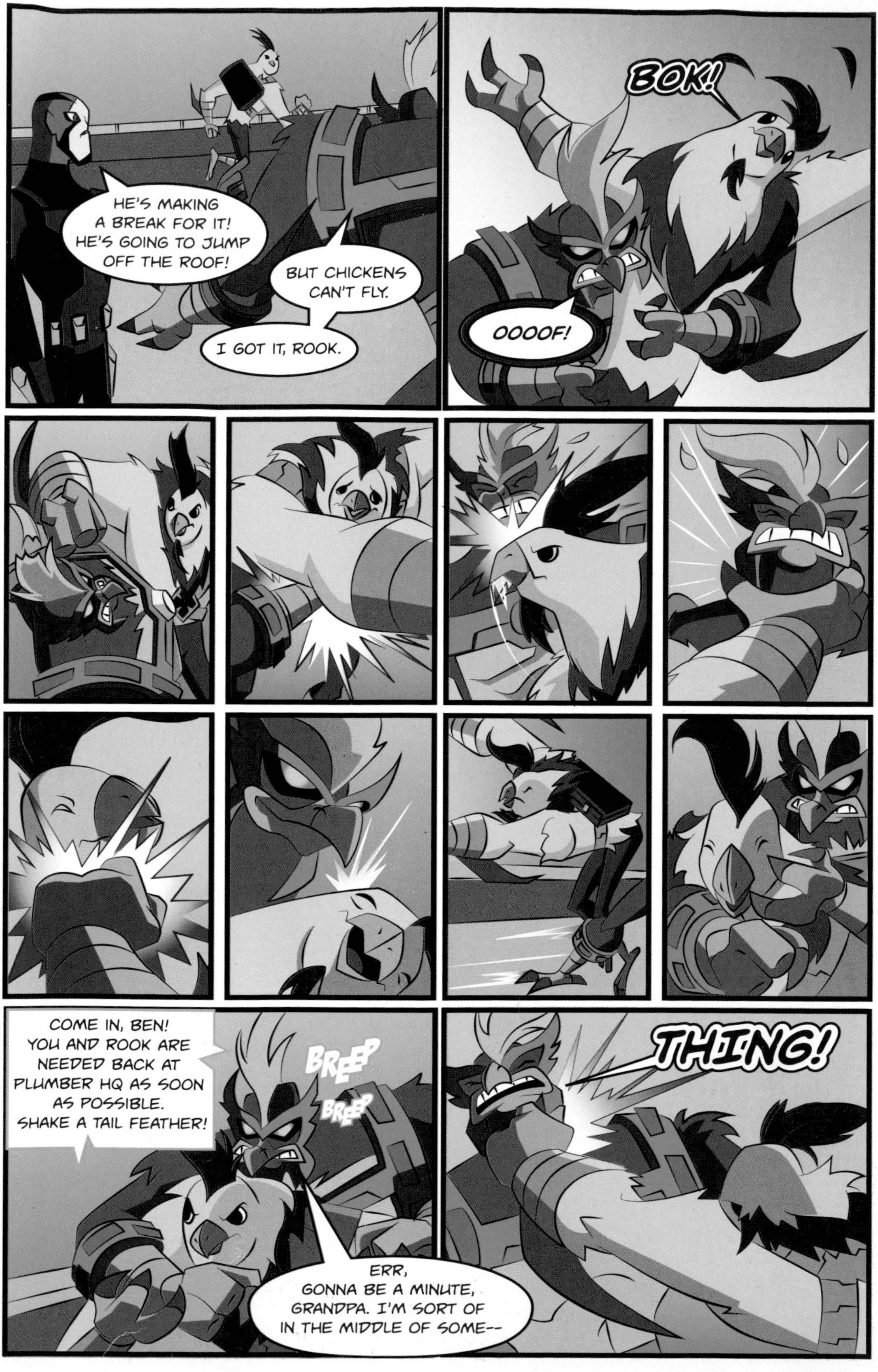
HE'S MAKING A BREAK FOR IT! HE'S GOING TO JUMP OFF THE ROOF!
BUT CHICKENS CAN'T FLY.
I GOT IT, ROOK.
BOK!
OOOOF!
COME IN, BEN! YOU AND ROOK ARE NEEDED BACK AT PLUMBER HQ AS SOON AS POSSIBLE. SHAKE A TAIL FEATHER!
BREEP
BREEP
ERR, GONNA BE A MINUTE, GRANDPA. I'M SORT OF IN THE MIDDLE OF SOME--
THING!

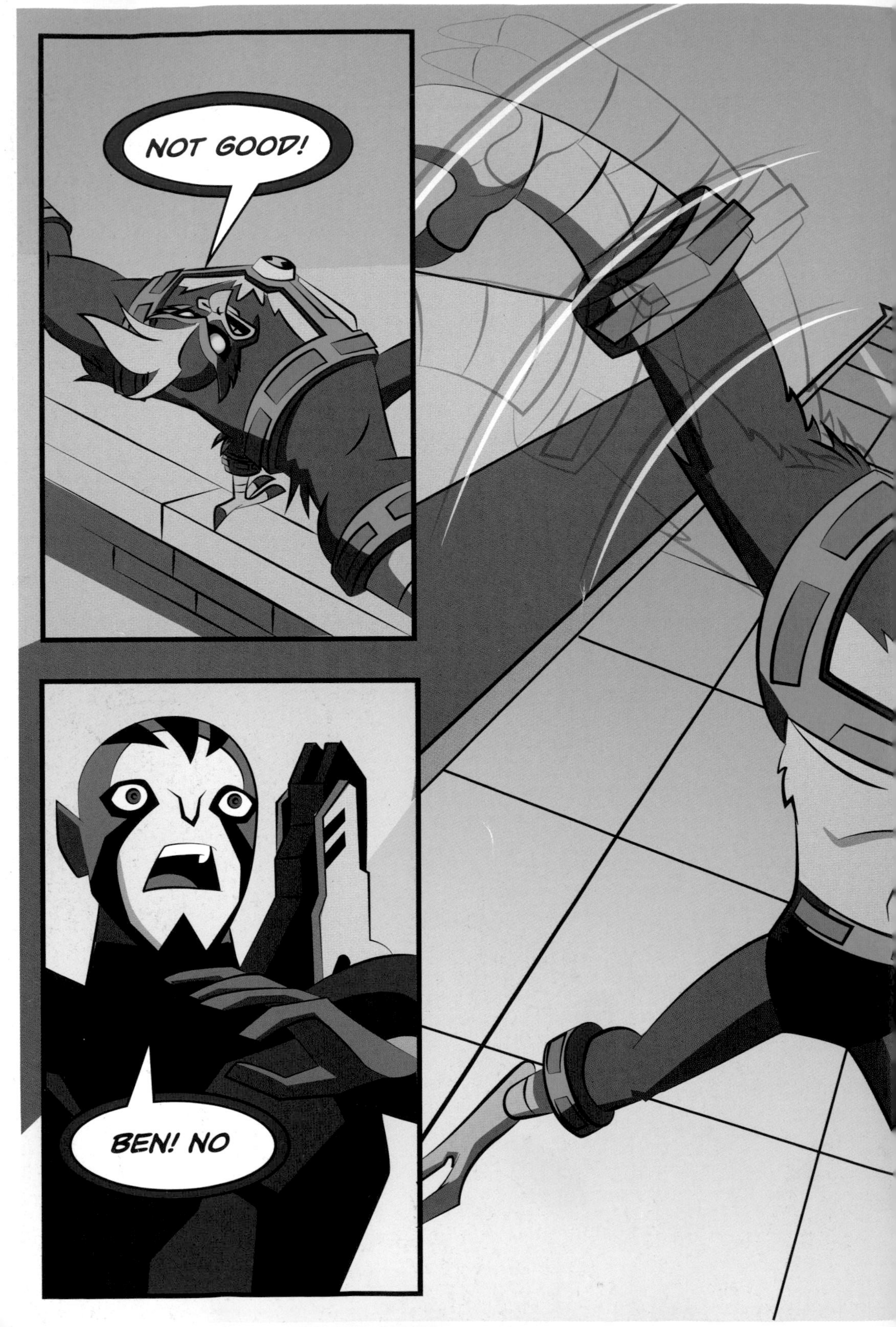
NOT GOOD!
BEN! NO

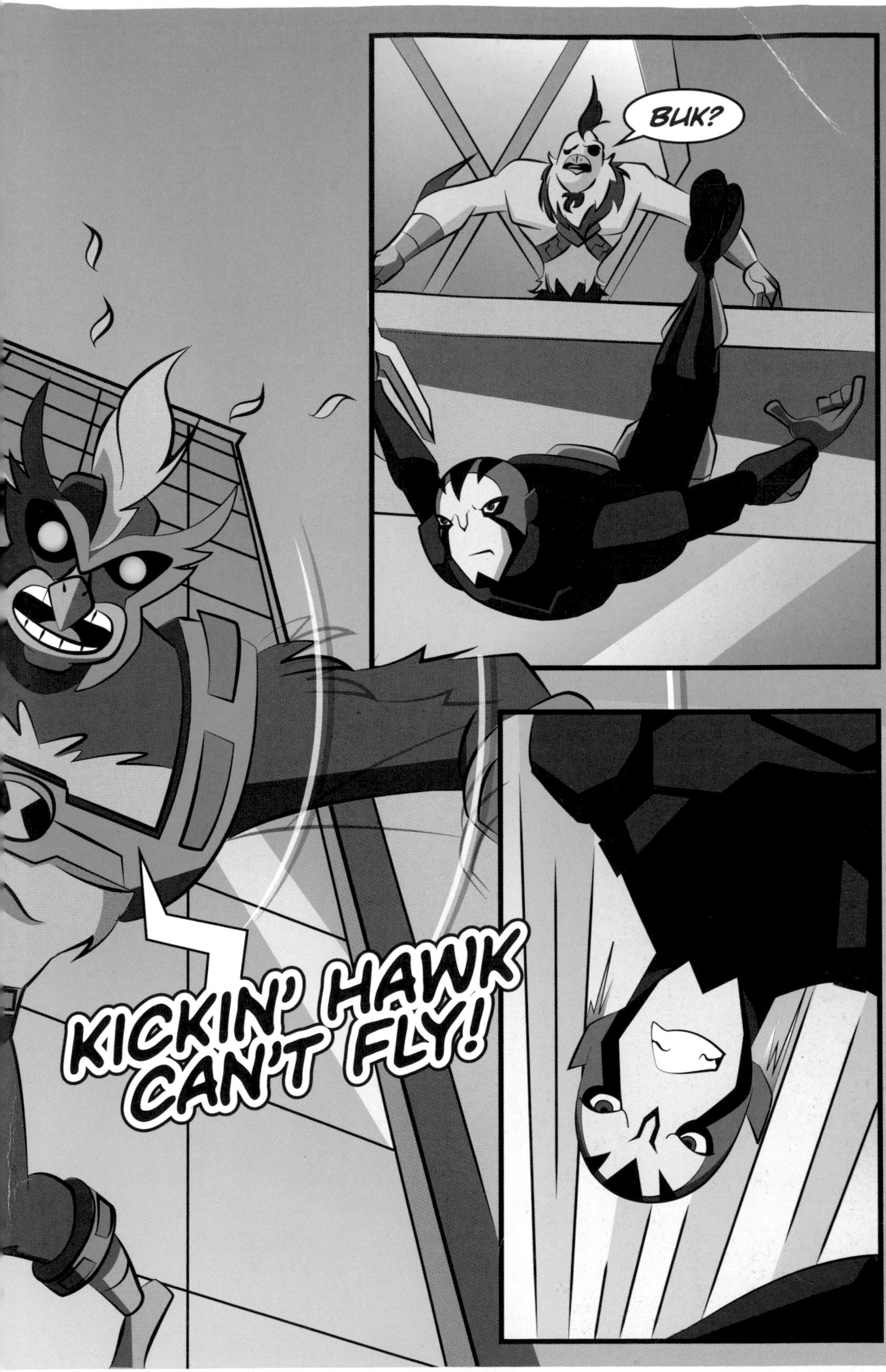
BUK?
KICKIN' HAWK CAN'T FLY!

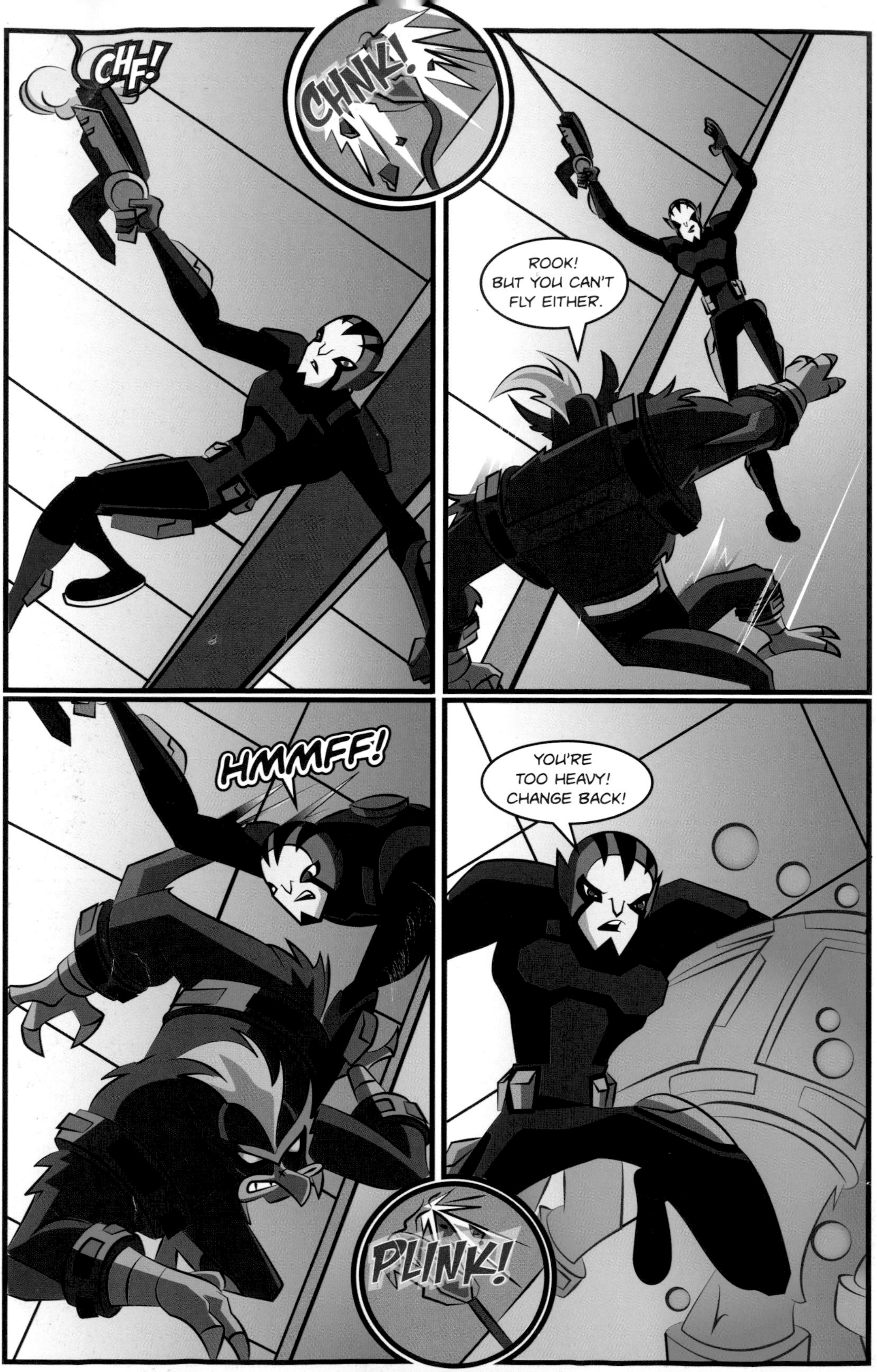
CHF!
CHNK!
ROOK! BUT YOU CAN'T FLY EITHER.
HMMFF!
YOU'RE TOO HEAVY! CHANGE BACK!
PLINK!

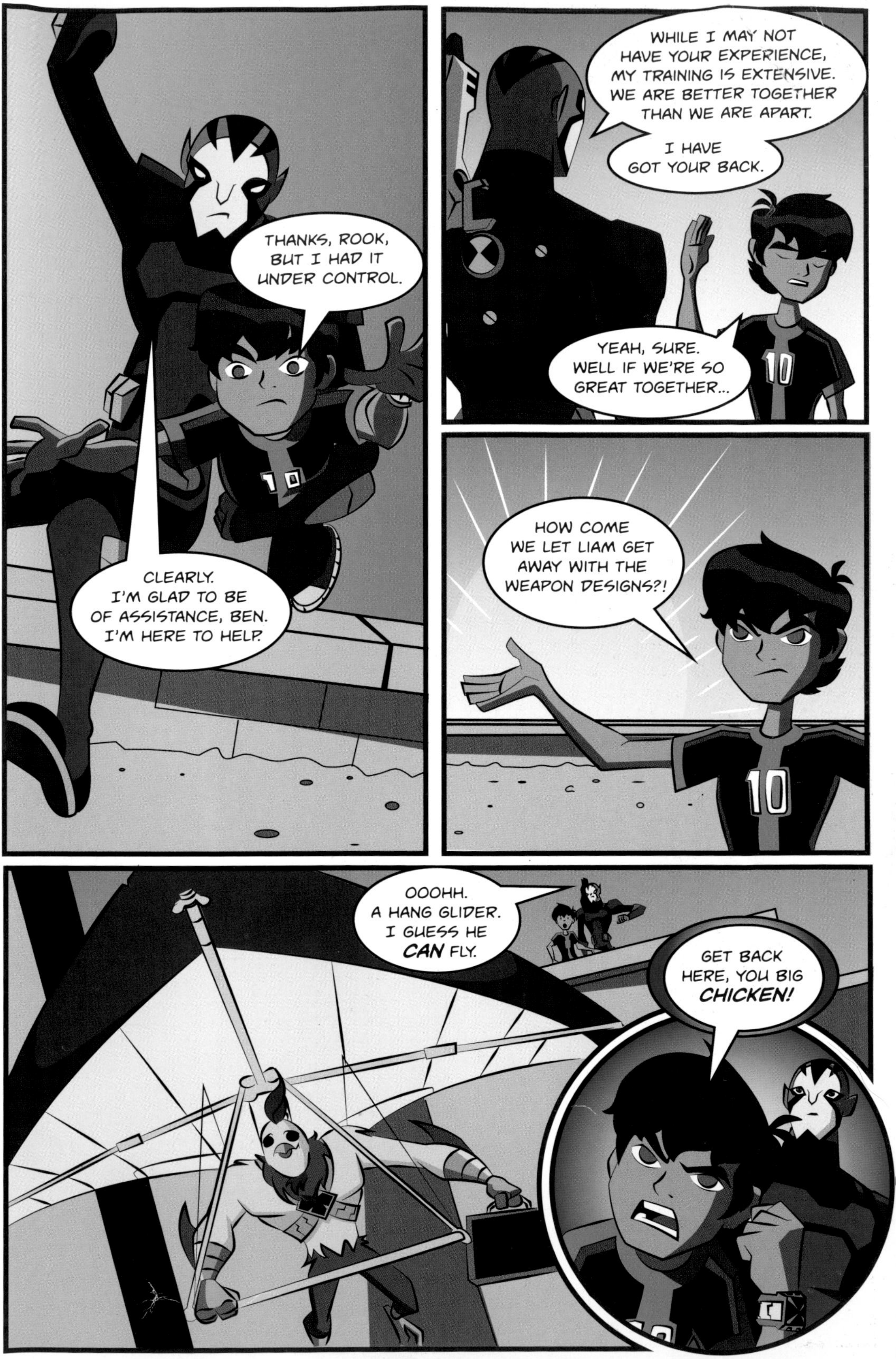
THANKS, ROOK, BUT I HAD IT UNDER CONTROL.
CLEARLY. I'M GLAD TO BE OF ASSISTANCE, BEN. I'M HERE TO HELP.
WHILE I MAY NOT HAVE YOUR EXPERIENCE, MY TRAINING IS EXTENSIVE. WE ARE BETTER TOGETHER THAN WE ARE APART.
I HAVE GOT YOUR BACK.
YEAH, SURE. WELL IF WE'RE SO GREAT TOGETHER...
HOW COME WE LET LIAM GET AWAY WITH THE WEAPON DESIGNS?!
OOOHH. A HANG GLIDER. I GUESS HE *CAN* FLY.
GET BACK HERE, YOU BIG ***CHICKEN!***

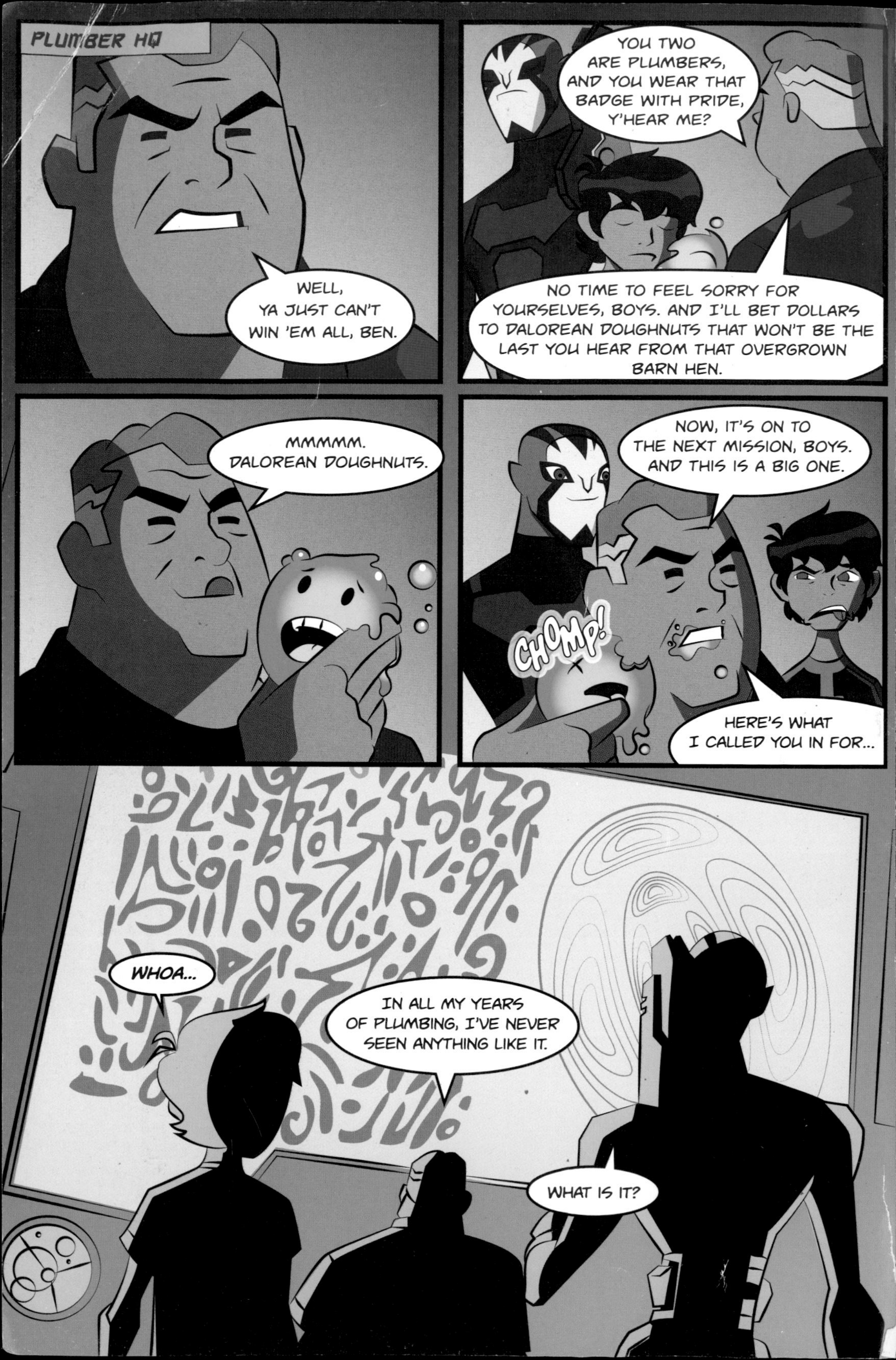
PLUMBER HQ
WELL, YA JUST CAN'T WIN 'EM ALL, BEN.
YOU TWO ARE PLUMBERS, AND YOU WEAR THAT BADGE WITH PRIDE, Y'HEAR ME?
NO TIME TO FEEL SORRY FOR YOURSELVES, BOYS. AND I'LL BET DOLLARS TO DALOREAN DOUGHNUTS THAT WON'T BE THE LAST YOU HEAR FROM THAT OVERGROWN BARN HEN.
MMMMM. DALOREAN DOUGHNUTS.
NOW, IT'S ON TO THE NEXT MISSION, BOYS. AND THIS IS A BIG ONE.
CHOMP!
HERE'S WHAT I CALLED YOU IN FOR...
WHOA...
IN ALL MY YEARS OF PLUMBING, I'VE NEVER SEEN ANYTHING LIKE IT.
WHAT IS IT?

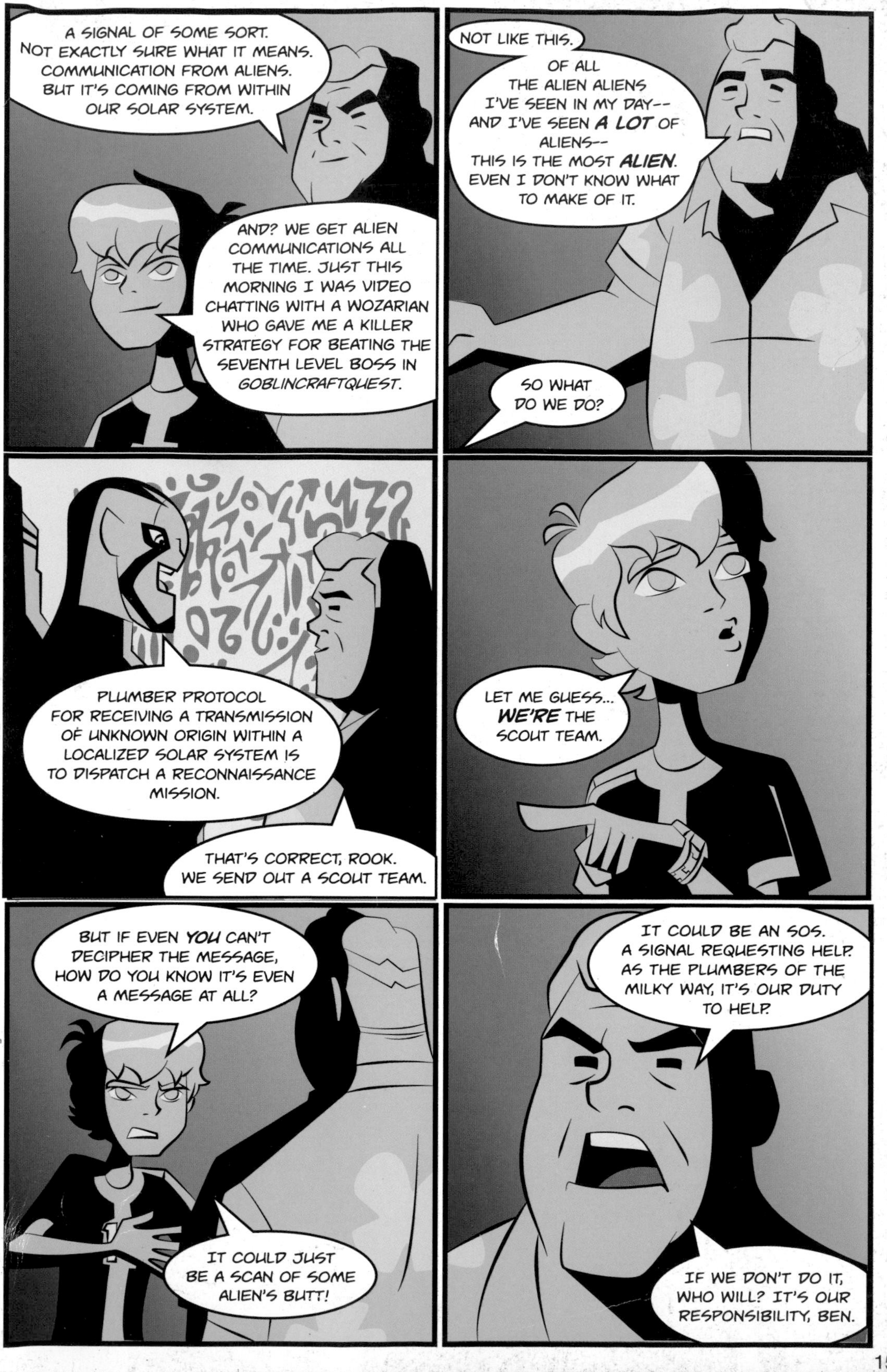
A SIGNAL OF SOME SORT. NOT EXACTLY SURE WHAT IT MEANS. COMMUNICATION FROM ALIENS. BUT IT'S COMING FROM WITHIN OUR SOLAR SYSTEM.
AND? WE GET ALIEN COMMUNICATIONS ALL THE TIME. JUST THIS MORNING I WAS VIDEO CHATTING WITH A WOZARIAN WHO GAVE ME A KILLER STRATEGY FOR BEATING THE SEVENTH LEVEL BOSS IN *GOBLINCRAFTQUEST*.
NOT LIKE THIS.
OF ALL THE ALIEN ALIENS I'VE SEEN IN MY DAY-- AND I'VE SEEN ***A LOT*** OF ALIENS-- THIS IS THE MOST ***ALIEN***. EVEN I DON'T KNOW WHAT TO MAKE OF IT.
SO WHAT DO WE DO?
PLUMBER PROTOCOL FOR RECEIVING A TRANSMISSION OF UNKNOWN ORIGIN WITHIN A LOCALIZED SOLAR SYSTEM IS TO DISPATCH A RECONNAISSANCE MISSION.
THAT'S CORRECT, ROOK. WE SEND OUT A SCOUT TEAM.
LET ME GUESS... ***WE'RE*** THE SCOUT TEAM.
BUT IF EVEN ***YOU*** CAN'T DECIPHER THE MESSAGE, HOW DO YOU KNOW IT'S EVEN A MESSAGE AT ALL?
IT COULD JUST BE A SCAN OF SOME ALIEN'S BUTT!
IT COULD BE AN SOS. A SIGNAL REQUESTING HELP. AS THE PLUMBERS OF THE MILKY WAY, IT'S OUR DUTY TO HELP.
IF WE DON'T DO IT, WHO WILL? IT'S OUR RESPONSIBILITY, BEN.

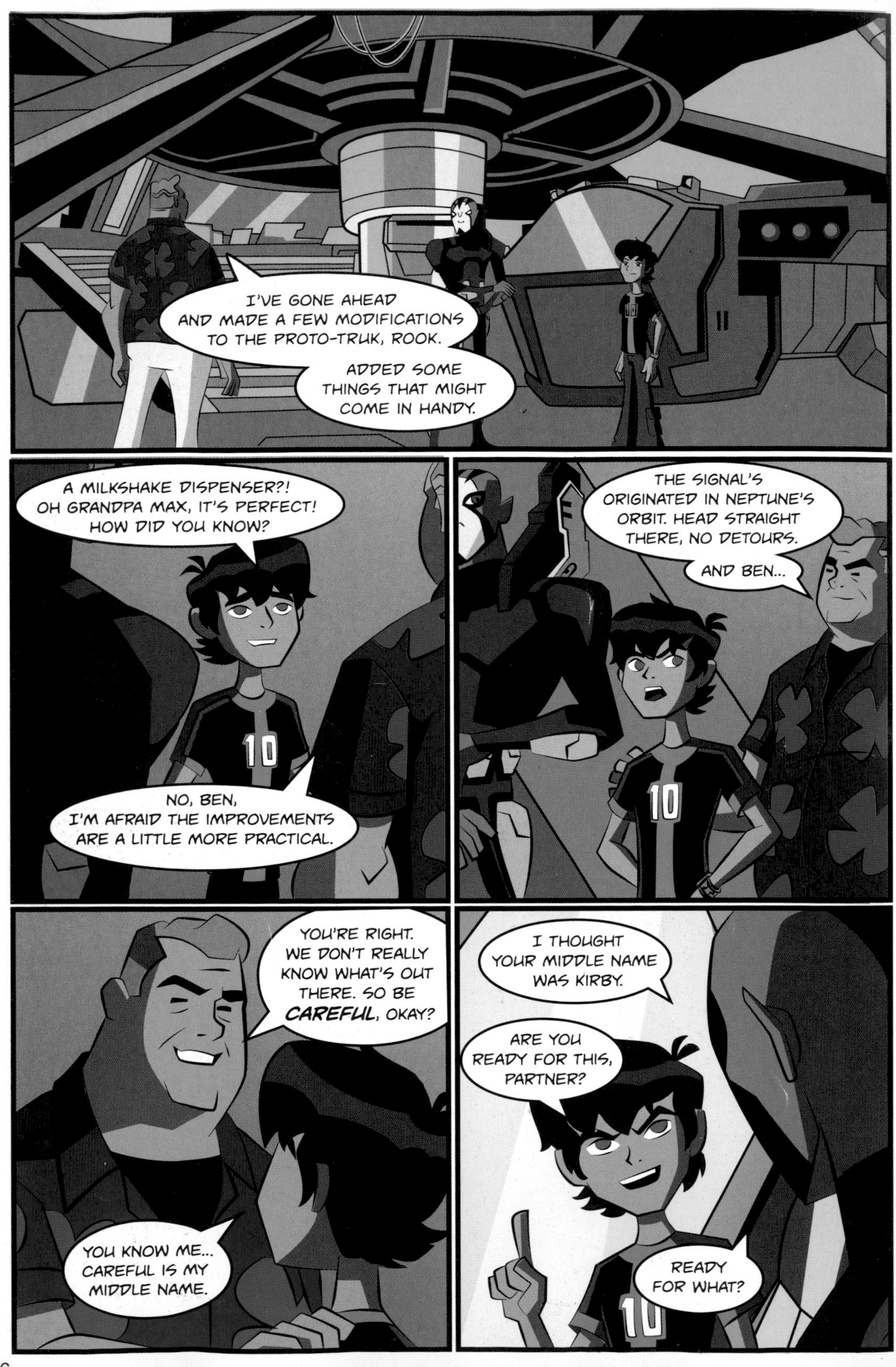
I'VE GONE AHEAD AND MADE A FEW MODIFICATIONS TO THE PROTO-TRUK, ROOK.
ADDED SOME THINGS THAT MIGHT COME IN HANDY.
A MILKSHAKE DISPENSER?! OH GRANDPA MAX, IT'S PERFECT! HOW DID YOU KNOW?
10
NO, BEN, I'M AFRAID THE IMPROVEMENTS ARE A LITTLE MORE PRACTICAL.
THE SIGNAL'S ORIGINATED IN NEPTUNE'S ORBIT. HEAD STRAIGHT THERE, NO DETOURS.
AND BEN...
10
YOU'RE RIGHT. WE DON'T REALLY KNOW WHAT'S OUT THERE. SO BE ***CAREFUL***, OKAY?
YOU KNOW ME... CAREFUL IS MY MIDDLE NAME.
I THOUGHT YOUR MIDDLE NAME WAS KIRBY.
ARE YOU READY FOR THIS, PARTNER?
READY FOR WHAT?
10

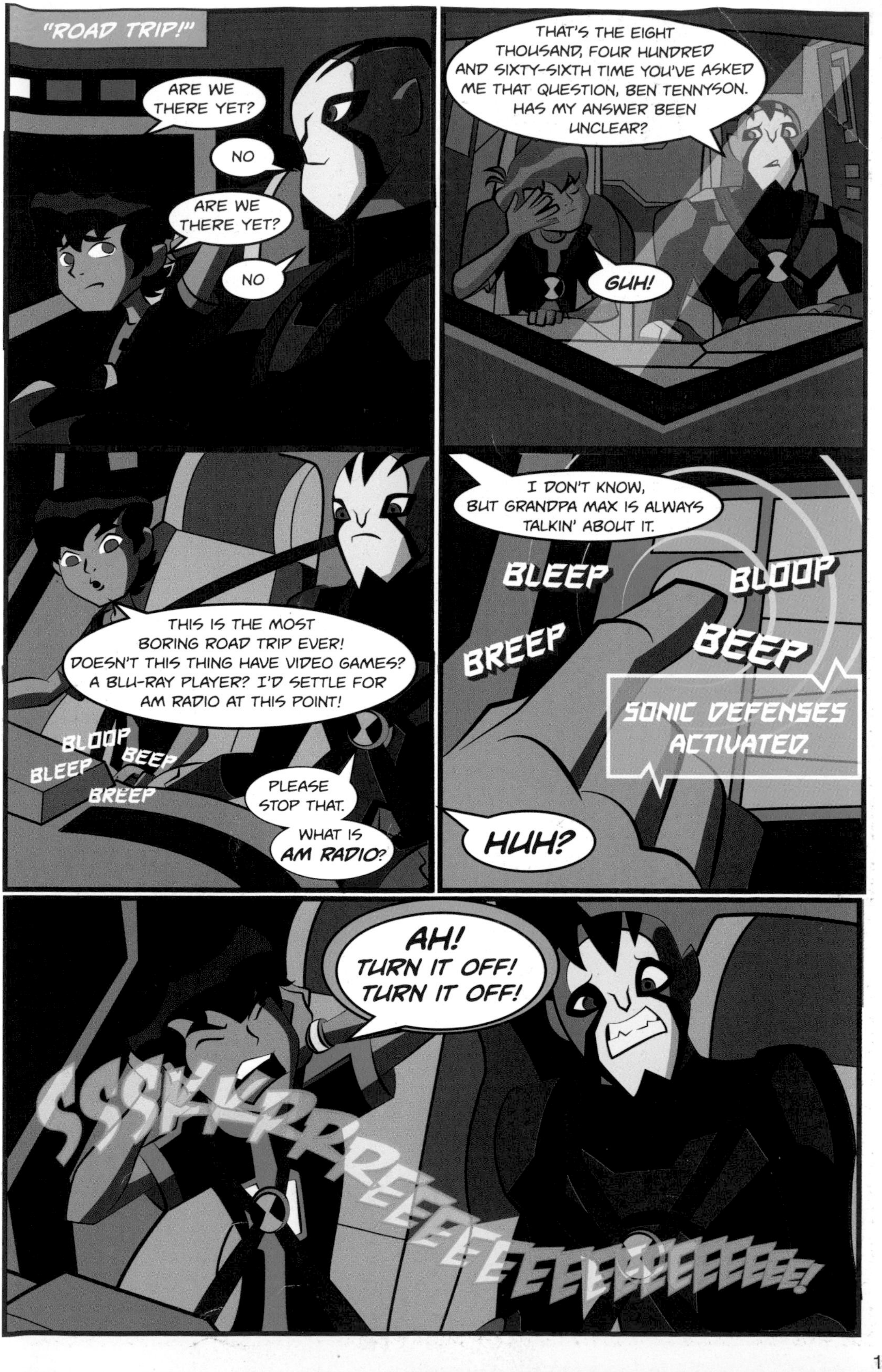
"ROAD TRIP!"
ARE WE THERE YET?
NO
ARE WE THERE YET?
NO
THAT'S THE EIGHT THOUSAND, FOUR HUNDRED AND SIXTY-SIXTH TIME YOU'VE ASKED ME THAT QUESTION, BEN TENNYSON. HAS MY ANSWER BEEN UNCLEAR?
GUH!
THIS IS THE MOST BORING ROAD TRIP EVER! DOESN'T THIS THING HAVE VIDEO GAMES? A BLU-RAY PLAYER? I'D SETTLE FOR AM RADIO AT THIS POINT!
BLOOP
BEEP
BLEEP
BREEP
PLEASE STOP THAT.
WHAT IS AM RADIO?
I DON'T KNOW, BUT GRANDPA MAX IS ALWAYS TALKIN' ABOUT IT.
BLEEP
BLOOP
BREEP
BEEP
SONIC DEFENSES ACTIVATED.
HUH?
AH! TURN IT OFF! TURN IT OFF!
SSSKKRRREEEEEEEEEEEEEEEEE!

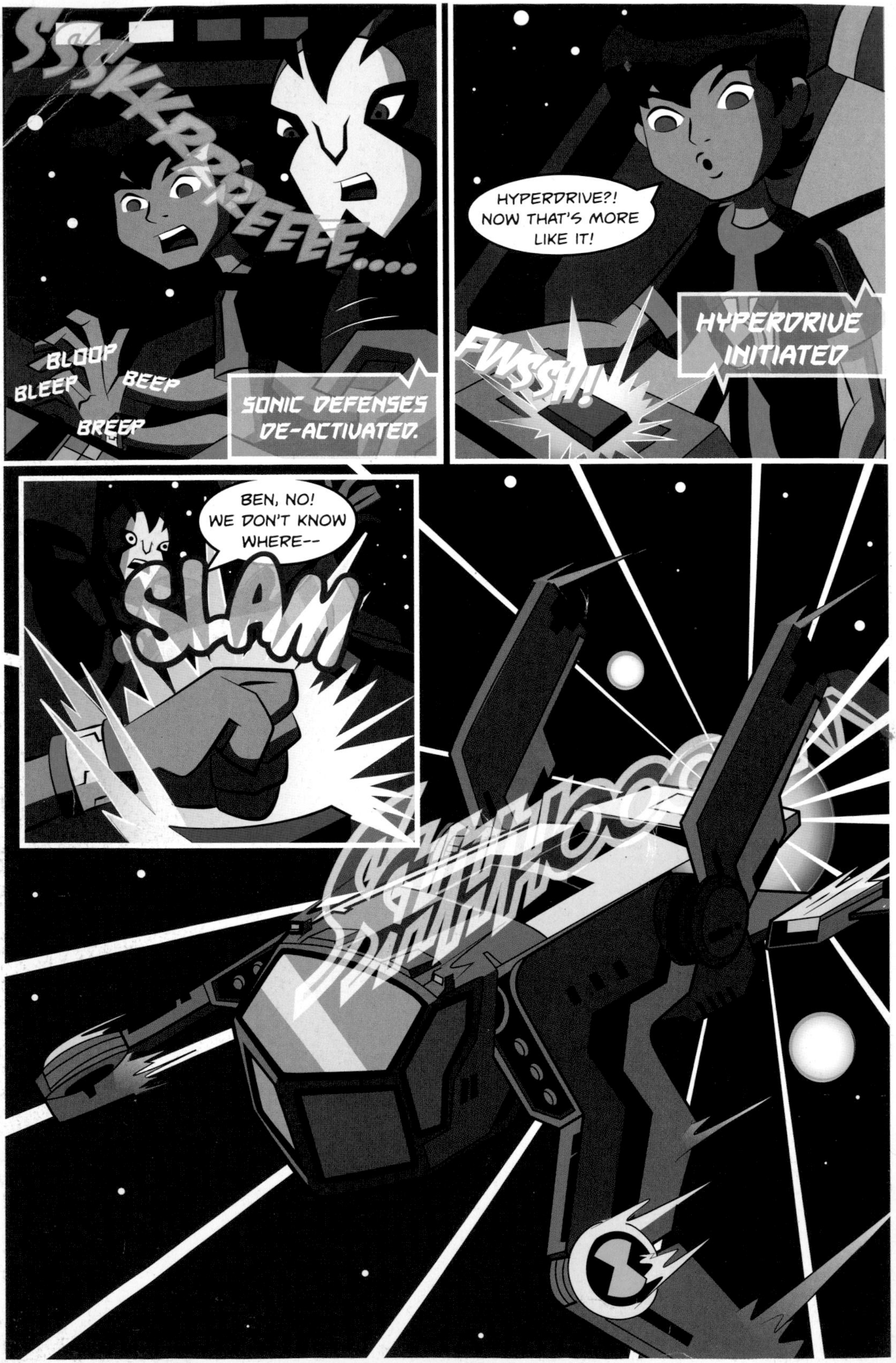
SSSKKRRREEEEE....
BLOOP
BLEEP
BEEP
BREEP
SONIC DEFENSES DE-ACTIVATED.
HYPERDRIVE?! NOW THAT'S MORE LIKE IT!
FWSSH!
HYPERDRIVE INITIATED
BEN, NO! WE DON'T KNOW WHERE--
SLAM

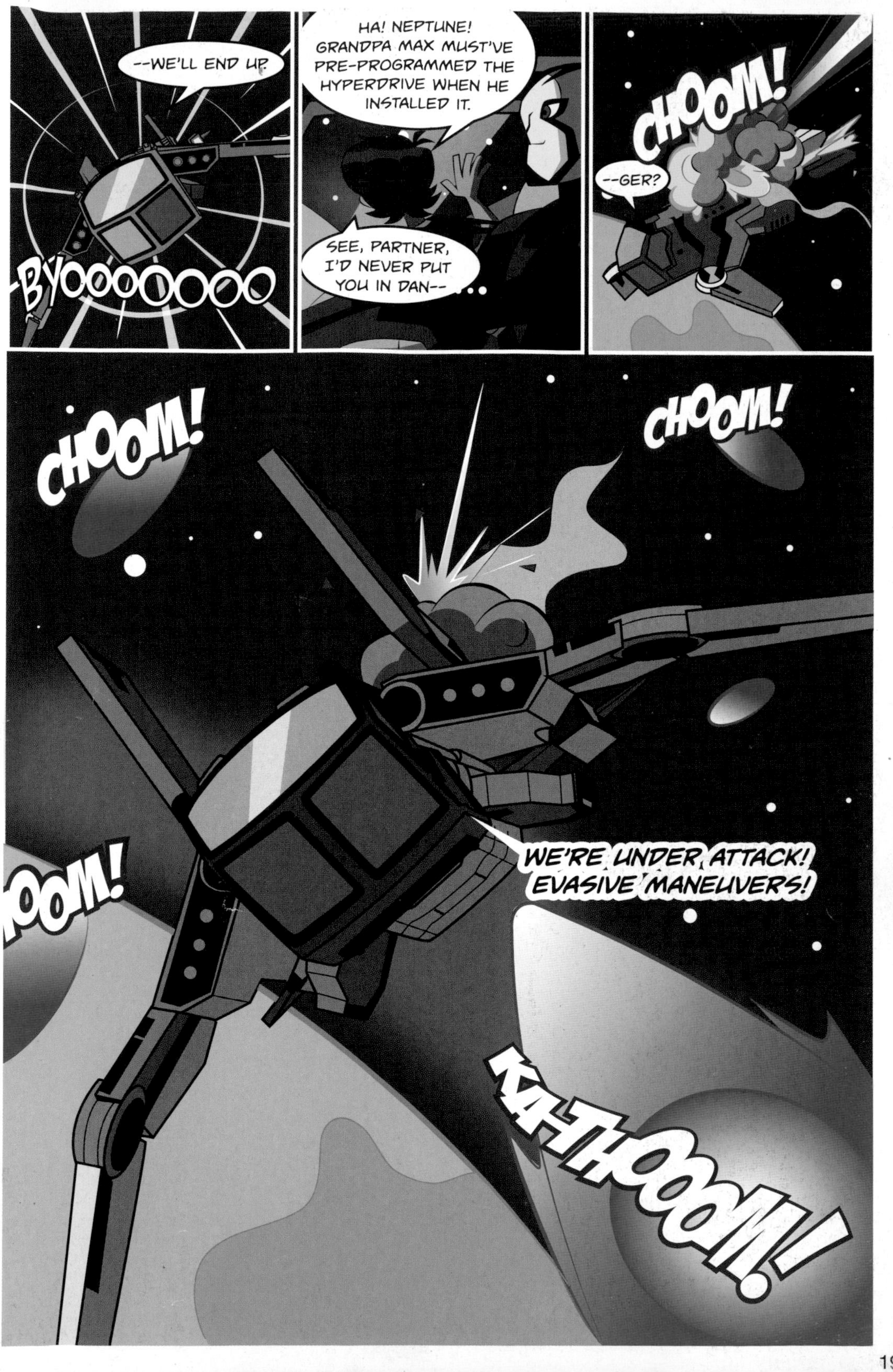
--WE'LL END UP.
BYOOOOOOO
HA! NEPTUNE! GRANDPA MAX MUST'VE PRE-PROGRAMMED THE HYPERDRIVE WHEN HE INSTALLED IT.
SEE, PARTNER, I'D NEVER PUT YOU IN DAN--
CHOOM!
--GER?
CHOOM!
CHOOM!
OOM!
WE'RE UNDER ATTACK! EVASIVE MANEUVERS!
KA-THOOOM!!

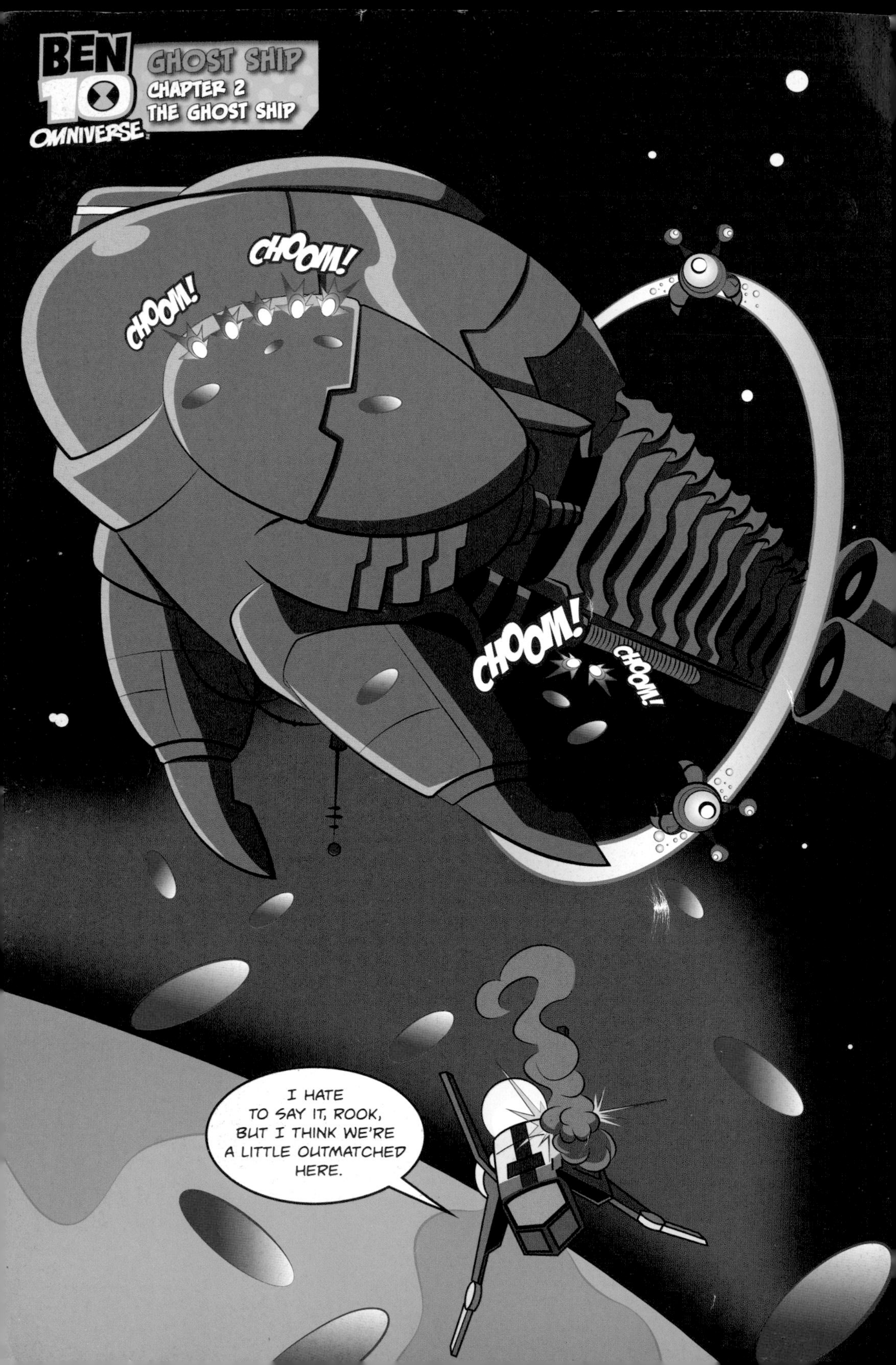
BEN 10 OMNIVERSE
GHOST SHIP
CHAPTER 2
THE GHOST SHIP
CHOOM!
CHOOM!
CHOOM!
CHOOM!
I HATE TO SAY IT, ROOK, BUT I THINK WE'RE A LITTLE OUTMATCHED HERE.

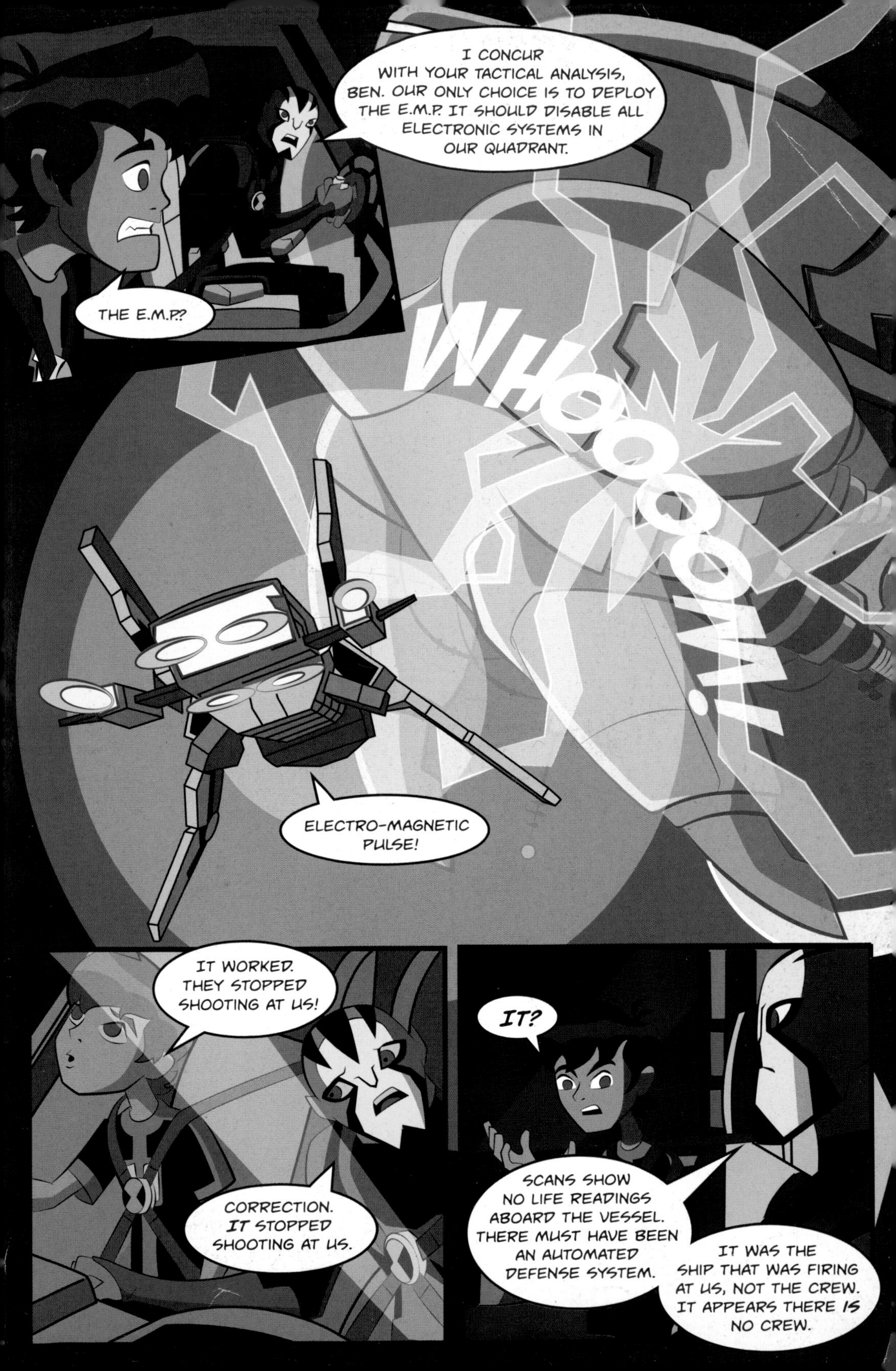

I CONCUR WITH YOUR TACTICAL ANALYSIS, BEN. OUR ONLY CHOICE IS TO DEPLOY THE E.M.P. IT SHOULD DISABLE ALL ELECTRONIC SYSTEMS IN OUR QUADRANT.
THE E.M.P.?
WHOOOOOM!
ELECTRO-MAGNETIC PULSE!
IT WORKED. THEY STOPPED SHOOTING AT US!
CORRECTION. *IT* STOPPED SHOOTING AT US.
IT?
SCANS SHOW NO LIFE READINGS ABOARD THE VESSEL. THERE MUST HAVE BEEN AN AUTOMATED DEFENSE SYSTEM.
IT WAS THE SHIP THAT WAS FIRING AT US, NOT THE CREW. IT APPEARS THERE *IS* NO CREW.

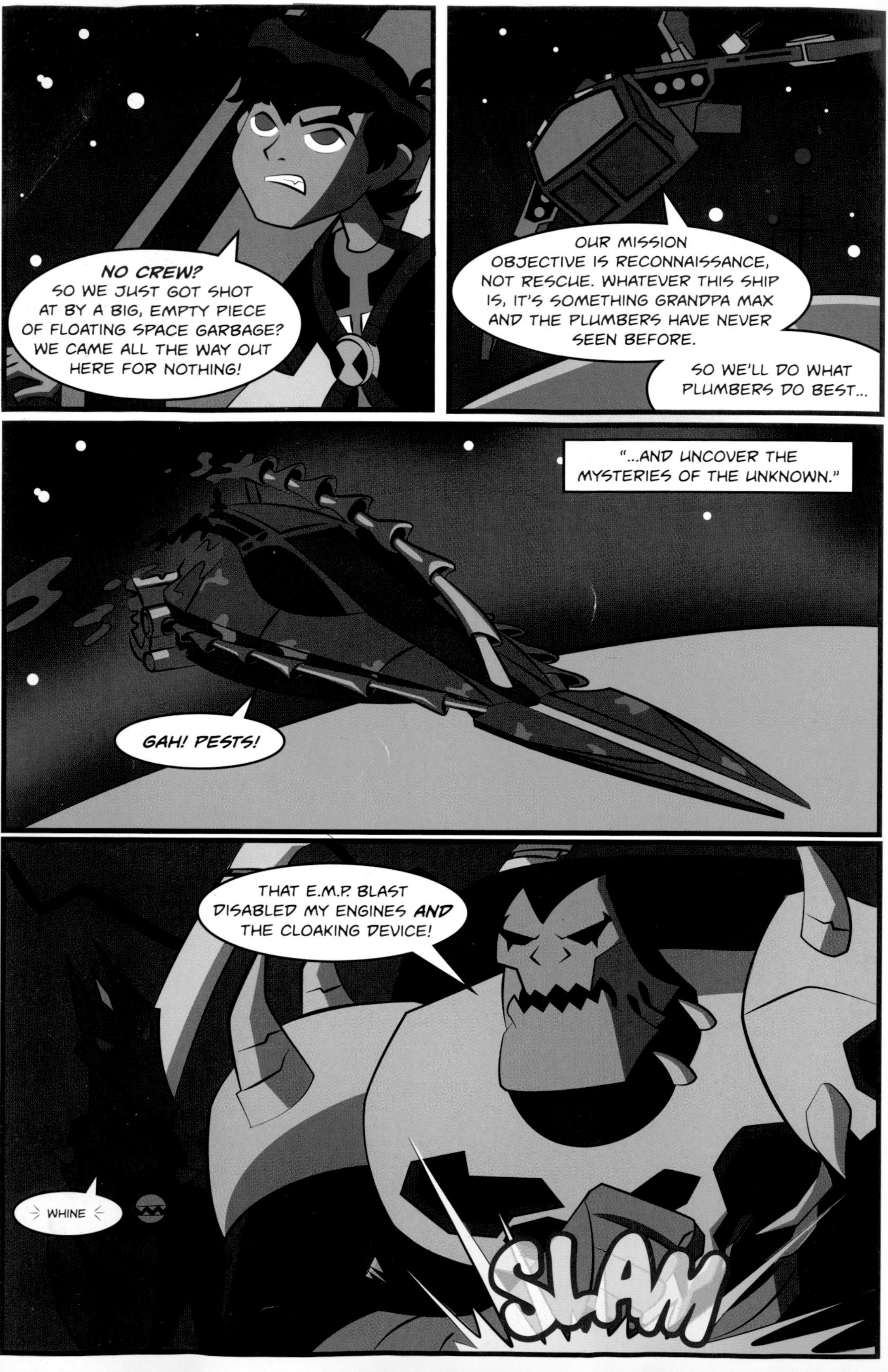
NO CREW? SO WE JUST GOT SHOT AT BY A BIG, EMPTY PIECE OF FLOATING SPACE GARBAGE? WE CAME ALL THE WAY OUT HERE FOR NOTHING!
OUR MISSION OBJECTIVE IS RECONNAISSANCE, NOT RESCUE. WHATEVER THIS SHIP IS, IT'S SOMETHING GRANDPA MAX AND THE PLUMBERS HAVE NEVER SEEN BEFORE.
SO WE'LL DO WHAT PLUMBERS DO BEST...
"...AND UNCOVER THE MYSTERIES OF THE UNKNOWN."
GAH! PESTS!
THAT E.M.P. BLAST DISABLED MY ENGINES AND THE CLOAKING DEVICE!
WHINE
SLAM

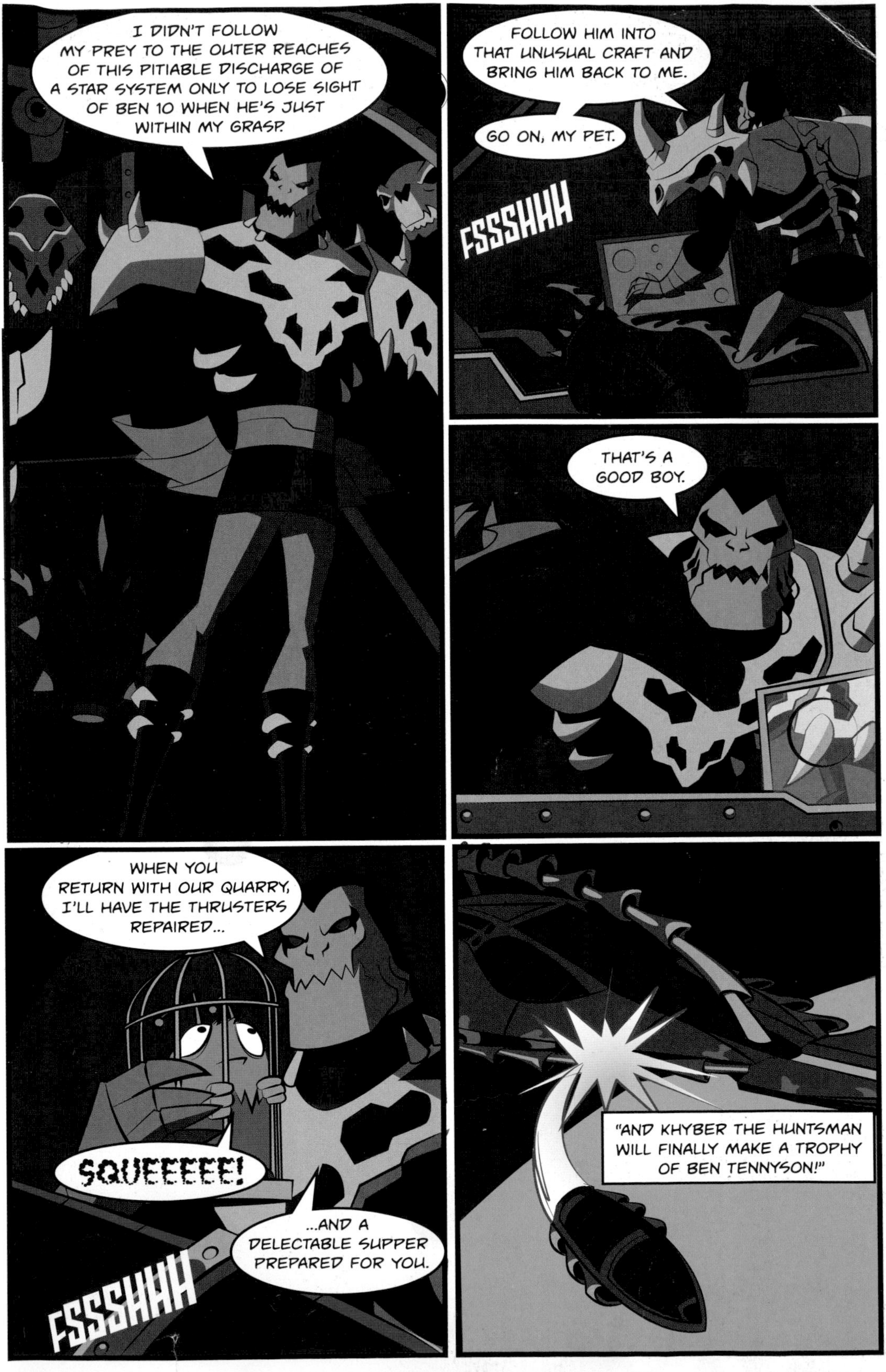

I DIDN'T FOLLOW MY PREY TO THE OUTER REACHES OF THIS PITIABLE DISCHARGE OF A STAR SYSTEM ONLY TO LOSE SIGHT OF BEN 10 WHEN HE'S JUST WITHIN MY GRASP.
FOLLOW HIM INTO THAT UNUSUAL CRAFT AND BRING HIM BACK TO ME.
GO ON, MY PET.
FSSSHHH
THAT'S A GOOD BOY.
WHEN YOU RETURN WITH OUR QUARRY, I'LL HAVE THE THRUSTERS REPAIRED...
SQUEEEEEE!
...AND A DELECTABLE SUPPER PREPARED FOR YOU.
FSSSHHH
"AND KHYBER THE HUNTSMAN WILL FINALLY MAKE A TROPHY OF BEN TENNYSON!"

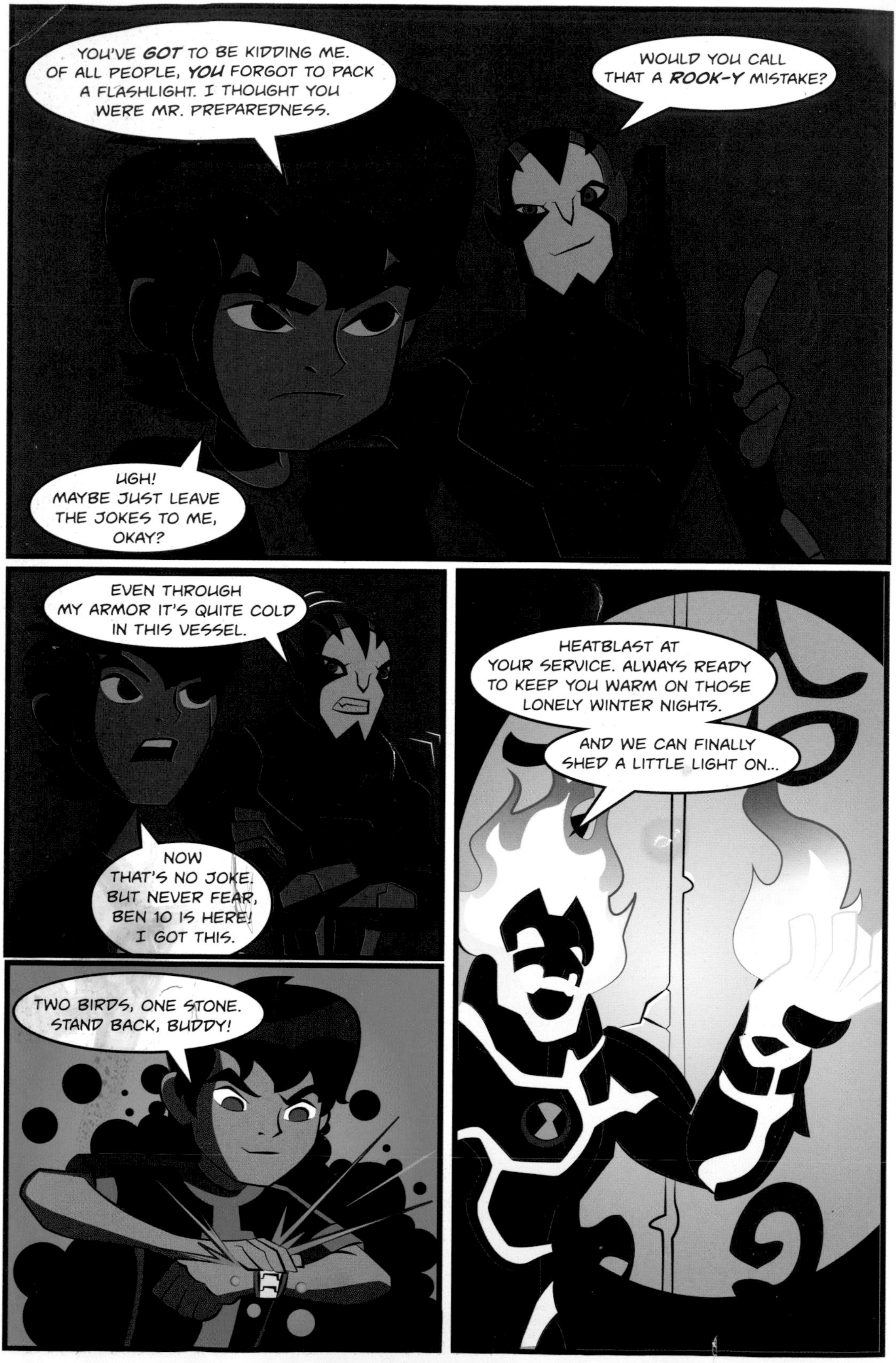
YOU'VE GOT TO BE KIDDING ME. OF ALL PEOPLE, YOU FORGOT TO PACK A FLASHLIGHT. I THOUGHT YOU WERE MR. PREPAREDNESS.
WOULD YOU CALL THAT A ROOK-Y MISTAKE?
UGH! MAYBE JUST LEAVE THE JOKES TO ME, OKAY?
EVEN THROUGH MY ARMOR IT'S QUITE COLD IN THIS VESSEL.
NOW THAT'S NO JOKE. BUT NEVER FEAR, BEN 10 IS HERE! I GOT THIS.
TWO BIRDS, ONE STONE. STAND BACK, BUDDY!
HEATBLAST AT YOUR SERVICE. ALWAYS READY TO KEEP YOU WARM ON THOSE LONELY WINTER NIGHTS.
AND WE CAN FINALLY SHED A LITTLE LIGHT ON...

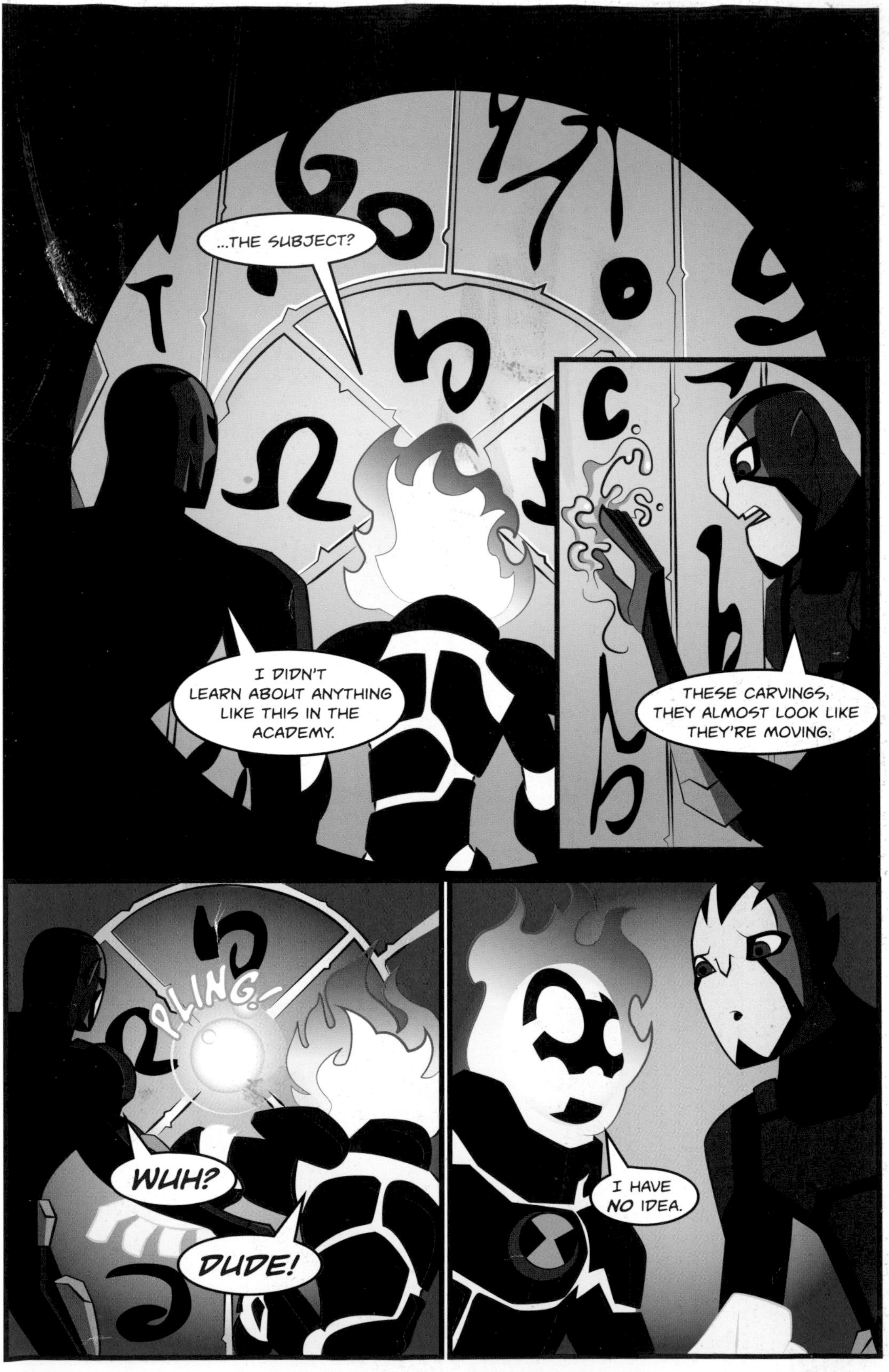
...THE SUBJECT?
I DIDN'T LEARN ABOUT ANYTHING LIKE THIS IN THE ACADEMY.
THESE CARVINGS, THEY ALMOST LOOK LIKE THEY'RE MOVING.
PLING!
WUH?
DUDE!
I HAVE NO IDEA.

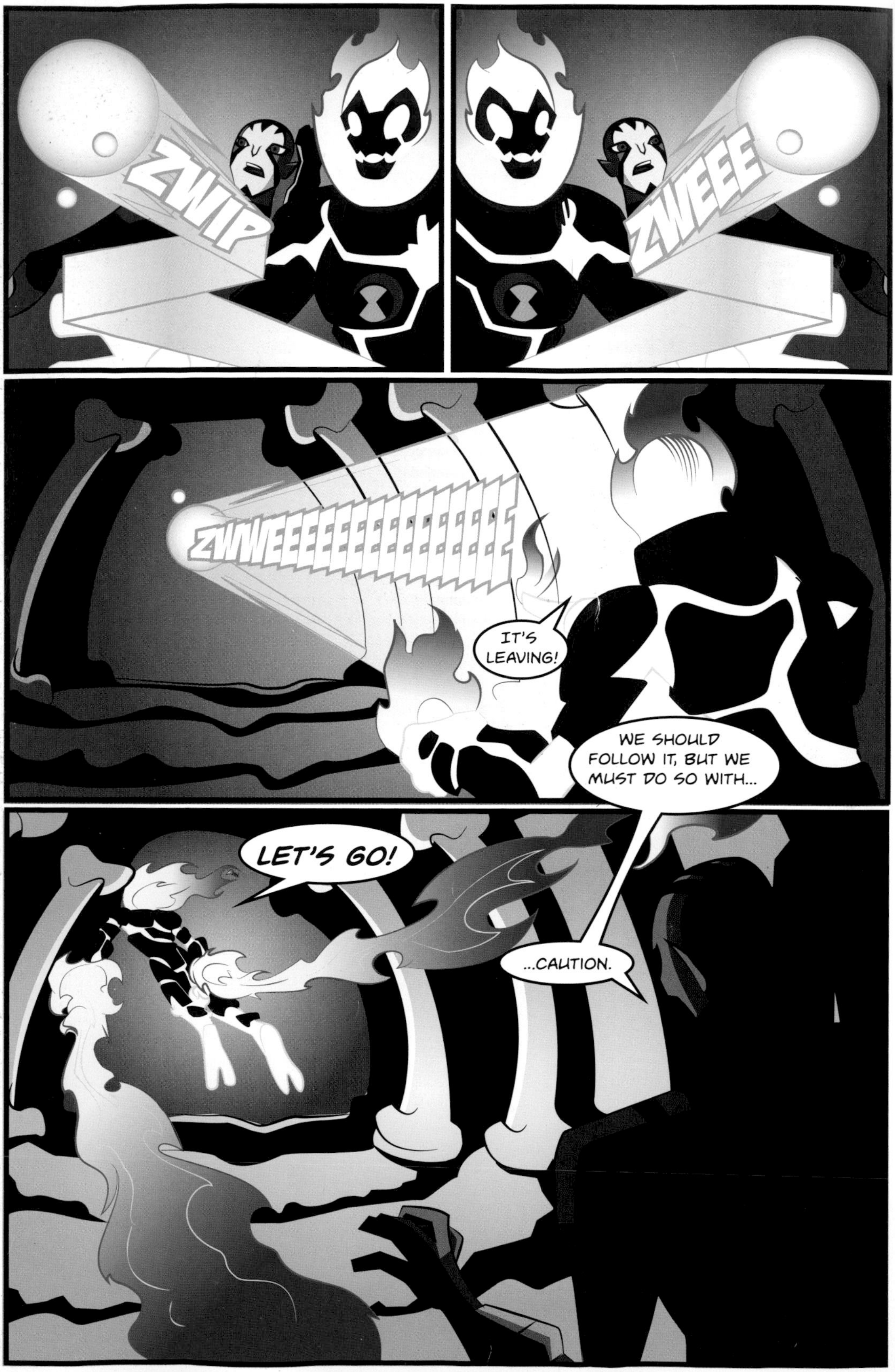
ZWIP
ZWEEE
ZWWEEEEEEEEEEEEEEE
IT'S LEAVING!
WE SHOULD FOLLOW IT, BUT WE MUST DO SO WITH...
LET'S GO!
...CAUTION.

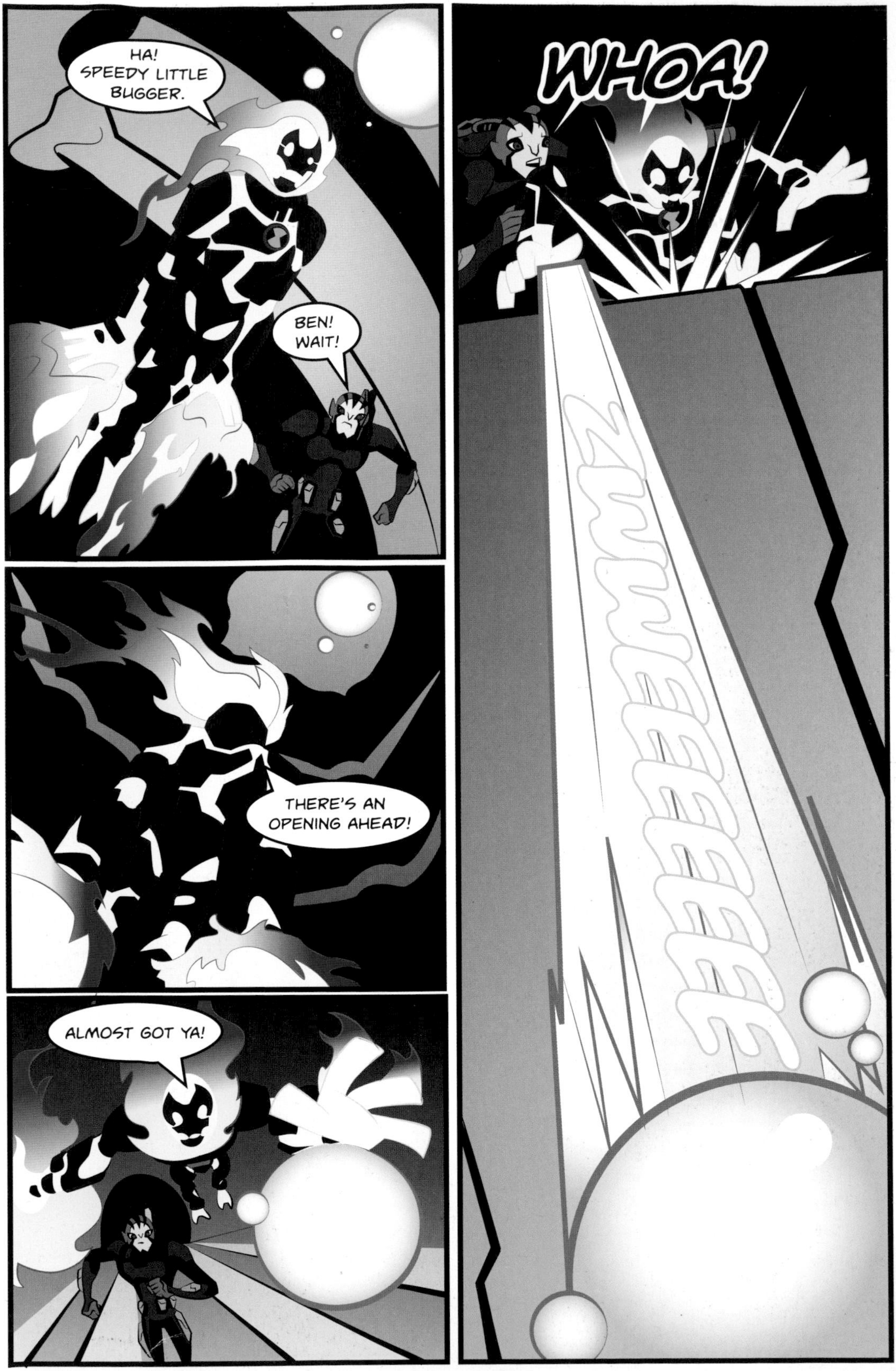
HA! SPEEDY LITTLE BUGGER.
BEN! WAIT!
THERE'S AN OPENING AHEAD!
ALMOST GOT YA!
WHOA!
ZWWEEEEEEE

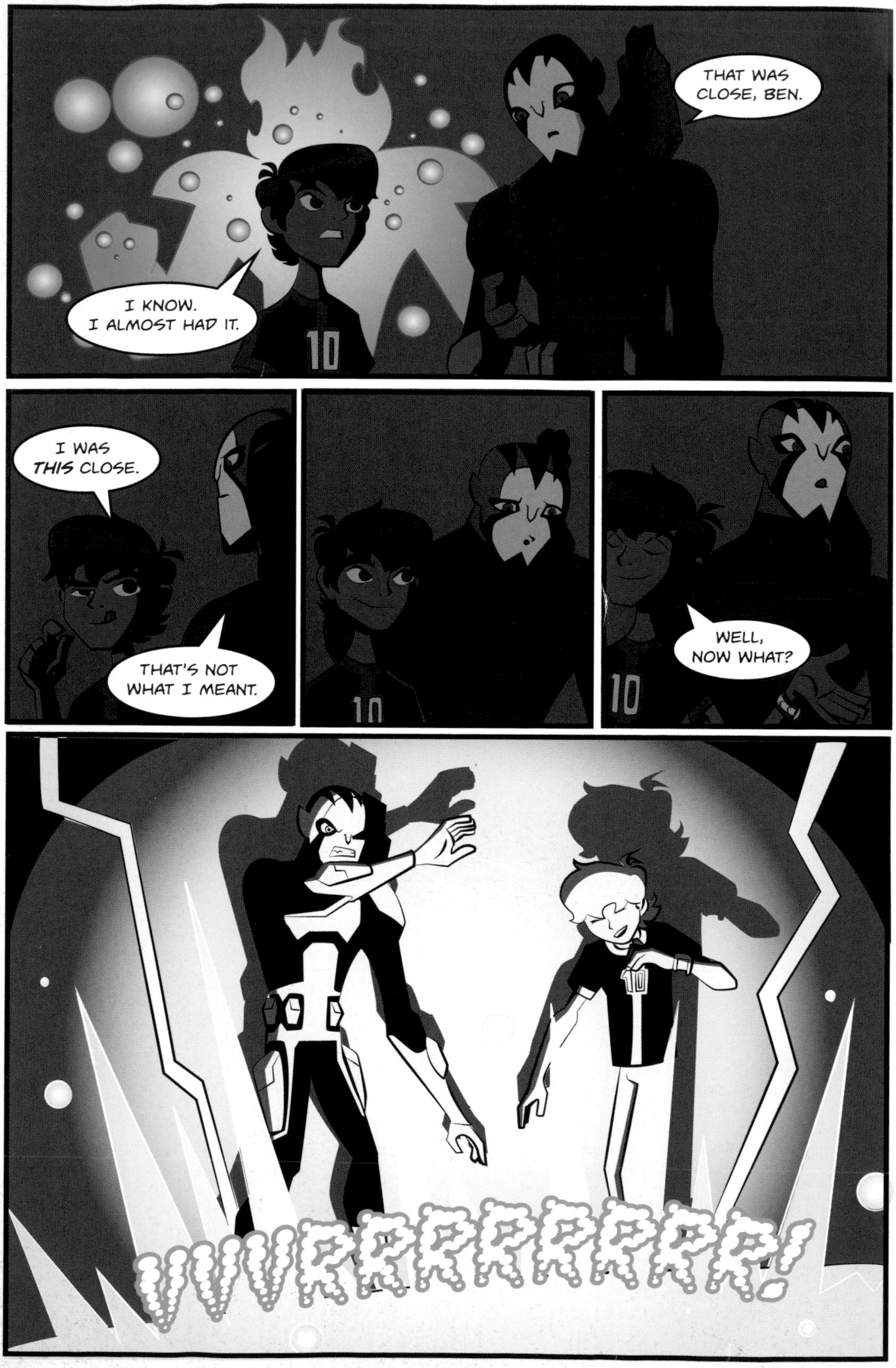
THAT WAS CLOSE, BEN.
I KNOW. I ALMOST HAD IT.
I WAS *THIS* CLOSE.
THAT'S NOT WHAT I MEANT.
WELL, NOW WHAT?
VVVRRRRRRRRR!

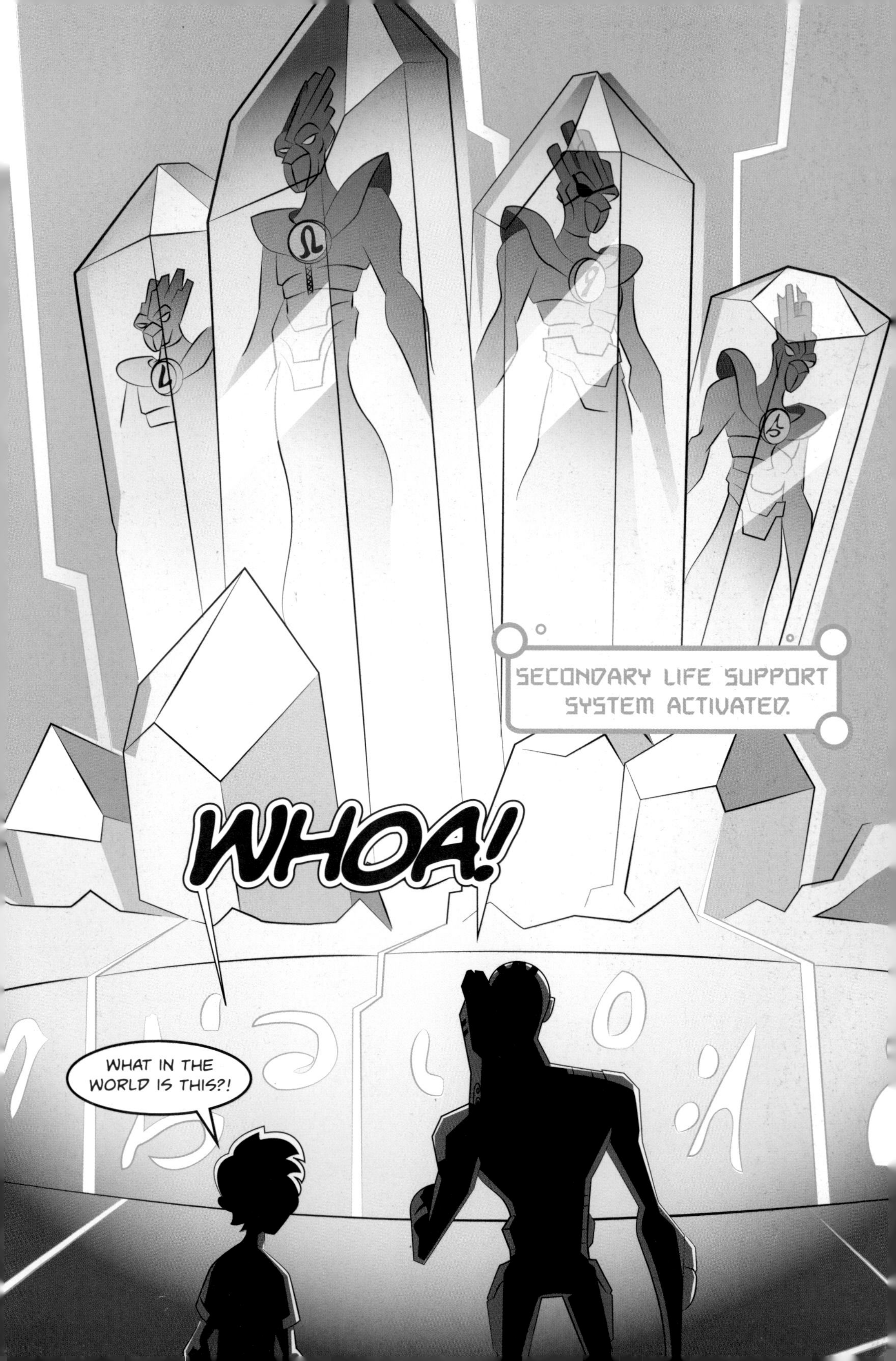
SECONDARY LIFE SUPPORT SYSTEM ACTIVATED.
WHOA!
WHAT IN THE WORLD IS THIS?!

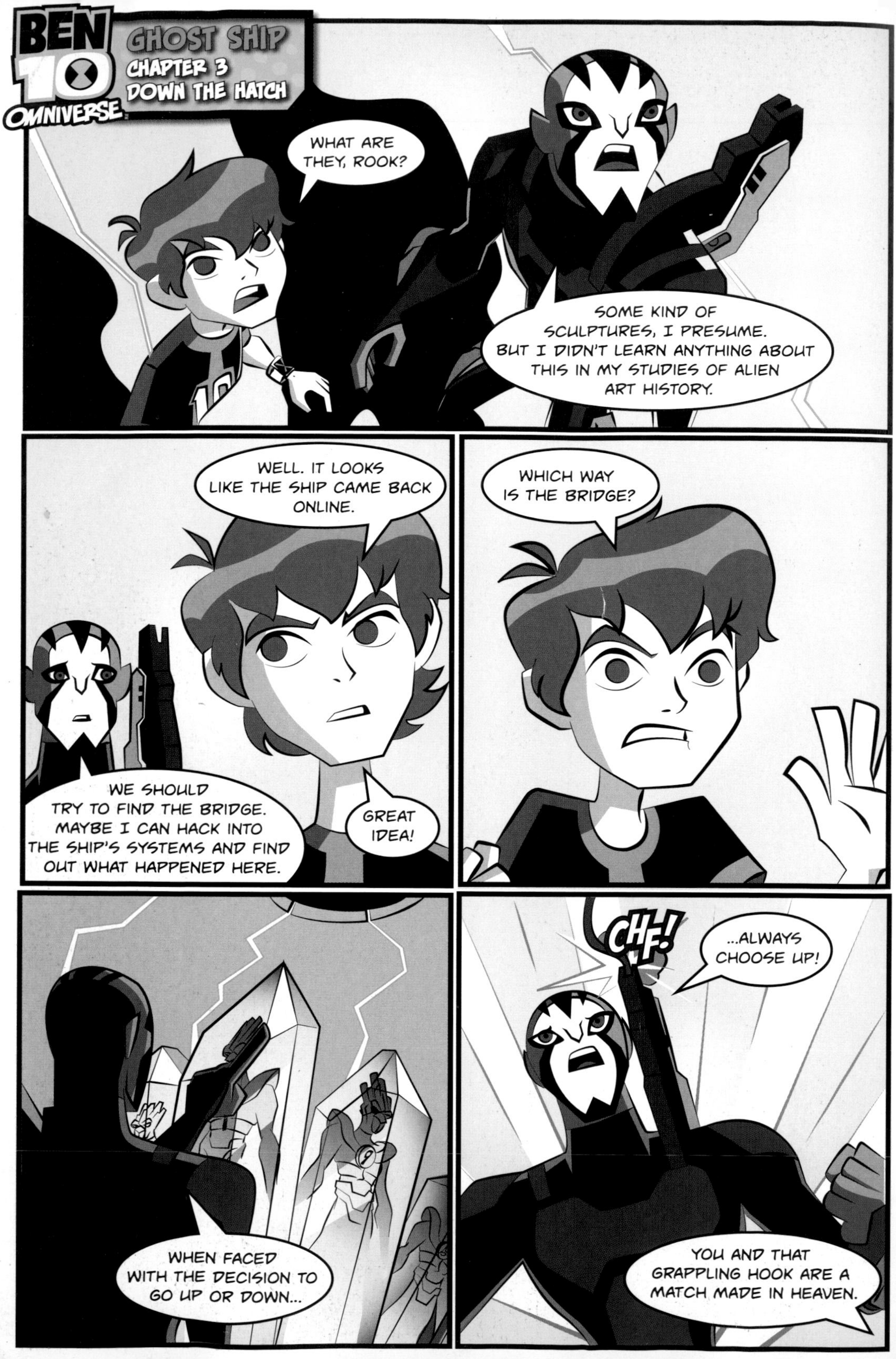
BEN 10 OMNIVERSE
GHOST SHIP
CHAPTER 3
DOWN THE HATCH
WHAT ARE THEY, ROOK?
SOME KIND OF SCULPTURES, I PRESUME. BUT I DIDN'T LEARN ANYTHING ABOUT THIS IN MY STUDIES OF ALIEN ART HISTORY.
WELL. IT LOOKS LIKE THE SHIP CAME BACK ONLINE.
WE SHOULD TRY TO FIND THE BRIDGE. MAYBE I CAN HACK INTO THE SHIP'S SYSTEMS AND FIND OUT WHAT HAPPENED HERE.
GREAT IDEA!
WHICH WAY IS THE BRIDGE?
WHEN FACED WITH THE DECISION TO GO UP OR DOWN...
CHF!
...ALWAYS CHOOSE UP!
YOU AND THAT GRAPPLING HOOK ARE A MATCH MADE IN HEAVEN.

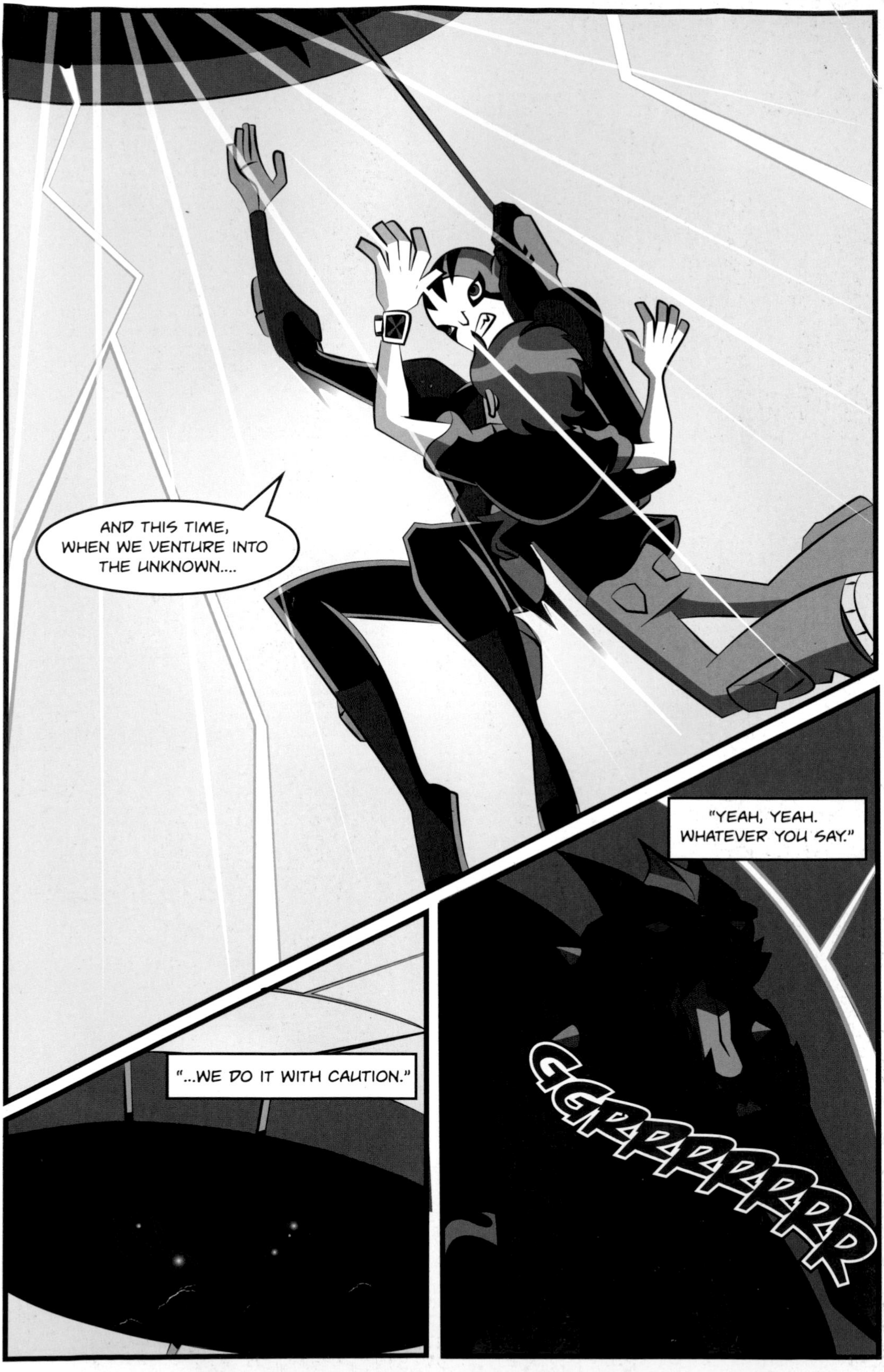
AND THIS TIME, WHEN WE VENTURE INTO THE UNKNOWN....
"YEAH, YEAH. WHATEVER YOU SAY."
"...WE DO IT WITH CAUTION."
GGRRRRRRRRR

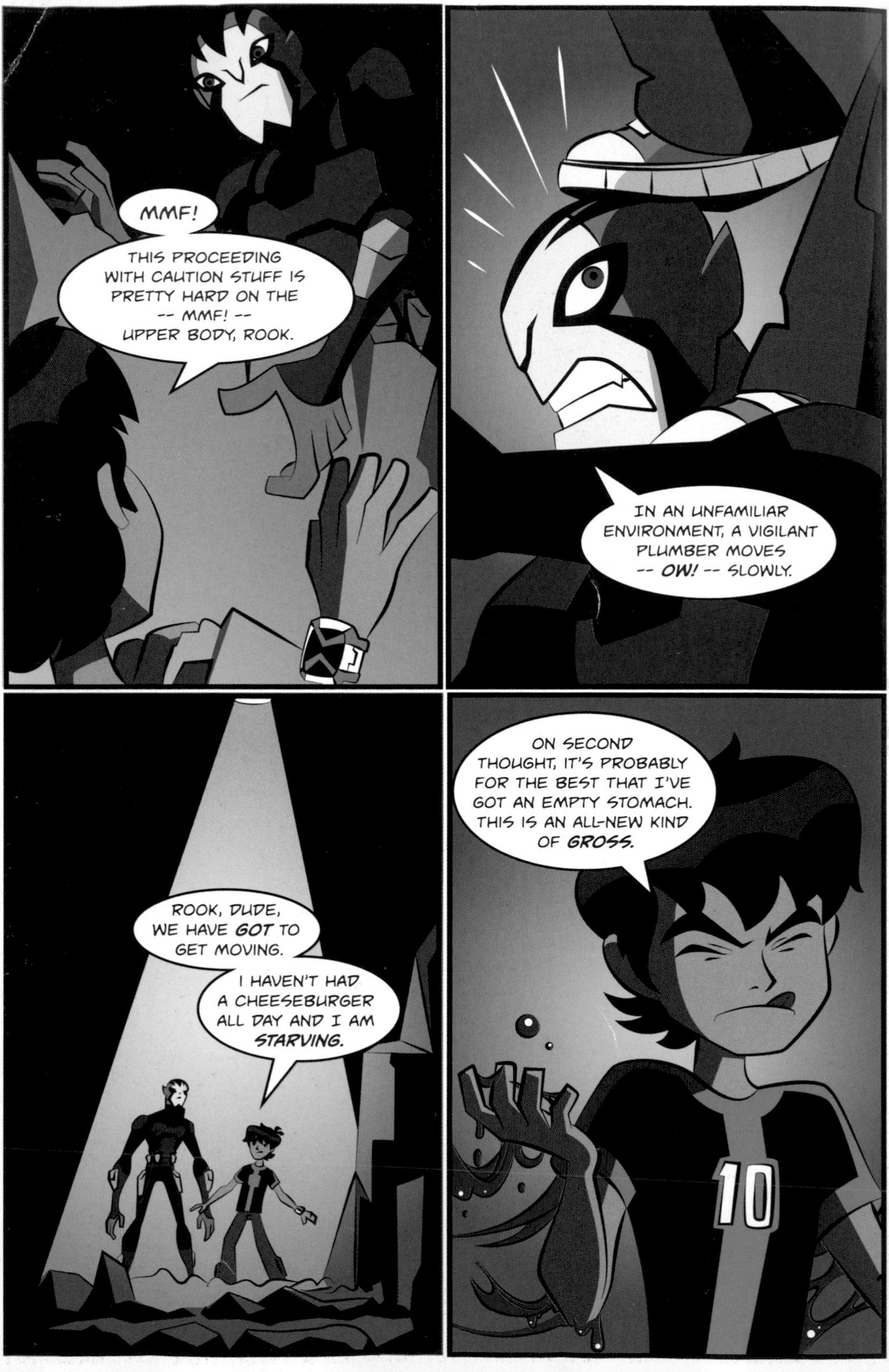
MMF!
THIS PROCEEDING WITH CAUTION STUFF IS PRETTY HARD ON THE -- MMF! -- UPPER BODY, ROOK.
IN AN UNFAMILIAR ENVIRONMENT, A VIGILANT PLUMBER MOVES -- *OW!* -- SLOWLY.
ROOK, DUDE, WE HAVE *GOT* TO GET MOVING.
I HAVEN'T HAD A CHEESEBURGER ALL DAY AND I AM *STARVING.*
ON SECOND THOUGHT, IT'S PROBABLY FOR THE BEST THAT I'VE GOT AN EMPTY STOMACH. THIS IS AN ALL-NEW KIND OF *GROSS.*
10

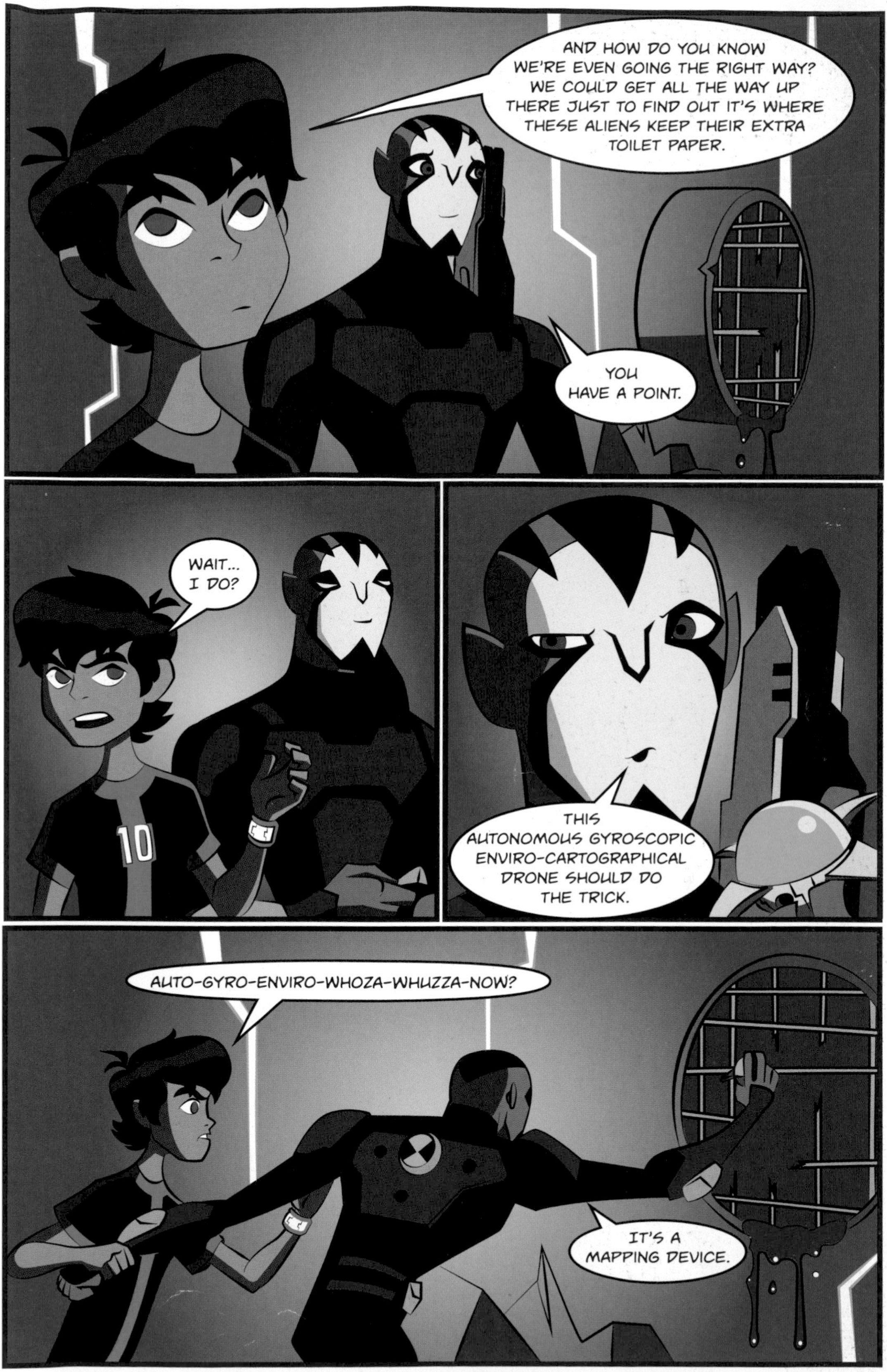
AND HOW DO YOU KNOW WE'RE EVEN GOING THE RIGHT WAY? WE COULD GET ALL THE WAY UP THERE JUST TO FIND OUT IT'S WHERE THESE ALIENS KEEP THEIR EXTRA TOILET PAPER.
YOU HAVE A POINT.
WAIT... I DO?
THIS AUTONOMOUS GYROSCOPIC ENVIRO-CARTOGRAPHICAL DRONE SHOULD DO THE TRICK.
AUTO-GYRO-ENVIRO-WHOZA-WHUZZA-NOW?
IT'S A MAPPING DEVICE.
10

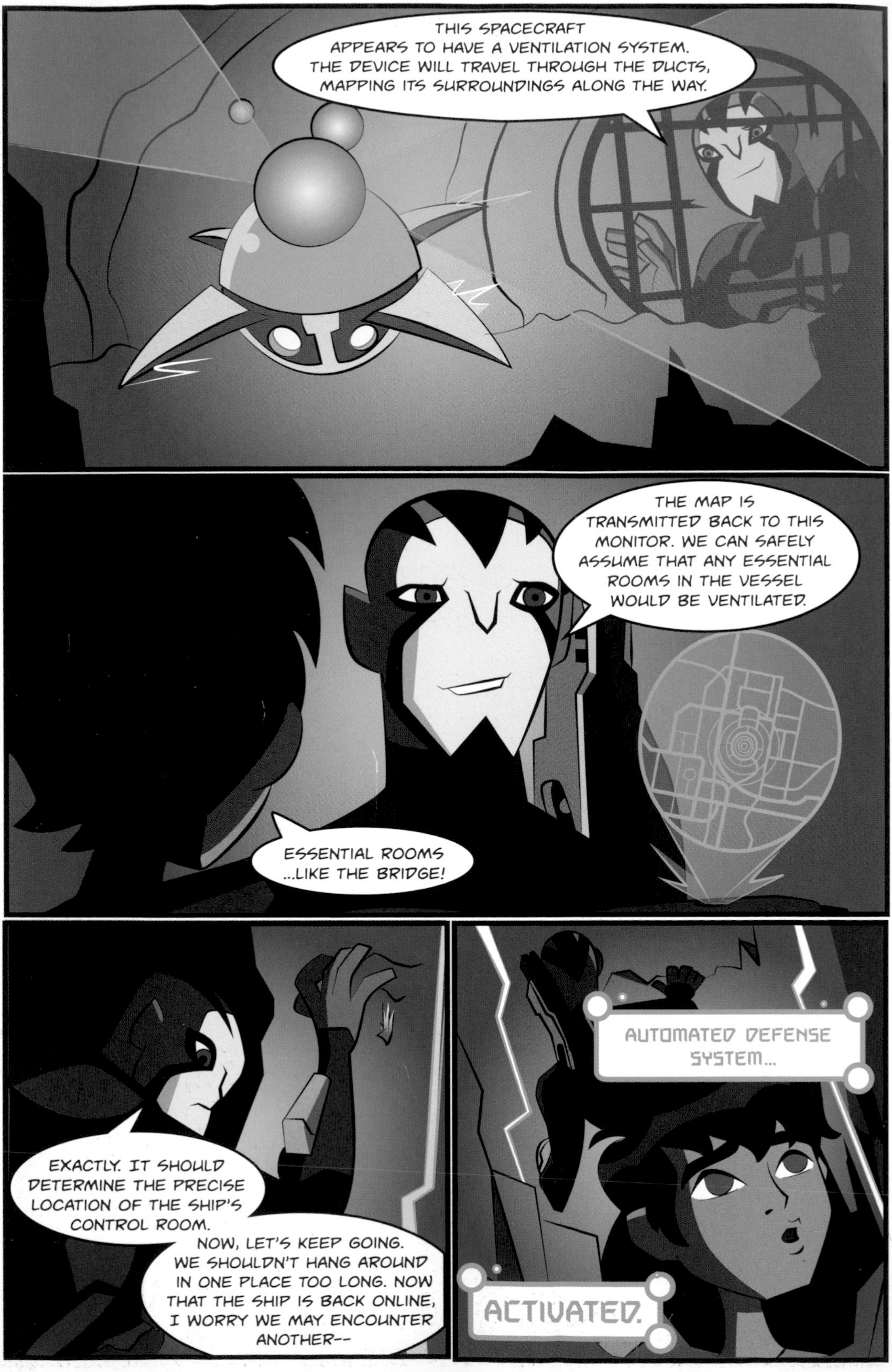
THIS SPACECRAFT APPEARS TO HAVE A VENTILATION SYSTEM. THE DEVICE WILL TRAVEL THROUGH THE DUCTS, MAPPING ITS SURROUNDINGS ALONG THE WAY.
THE MAP IS TRANSMITTED BACK TO THIS MONITOR. WE CAN SAFELY ASSUME THAT ANY ESSENTIAL ROOMS IN THE VESSEL WOULD BE VENTILATED.
ESSENTIAL ROOMS ...LIKE THE BRIDGE!
EXACTLY. IT SHOULD DETERMINE THE PRECISE LOCATION OF THE SHIP'S CONTROL ROOM.
NOW, LET'S KEEP GOING. WE SHOULDN'T HANG AROUND IN ONE PLACE TOO LONG. NOW THAT THE SHIP IS BACK ONLINE, I WORRY WE MAY ENCOUNTER ANOTHER--
AUTOMATED DEFENSE SYSTEM...
ACTIVATED.

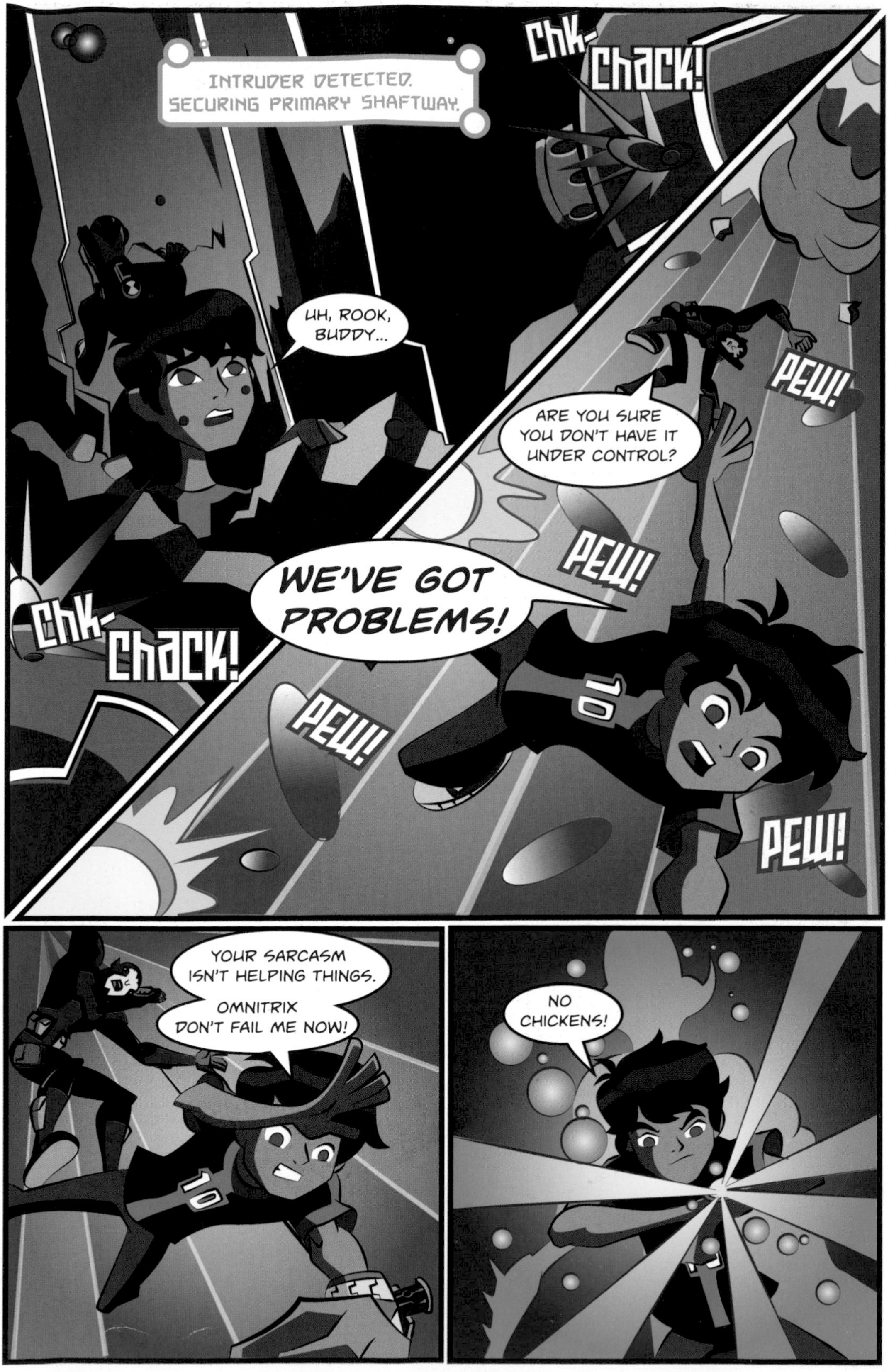
INTRUDER DETECTED. SECURING PRIMARY SHAFTWAY.
CHK-CHACK!
UH, ROOK, BUDDY...
ARE YOU SURE YOU DON'T HAVE IT UNDER CONTROL?
PEW!
PEW!
WE'VE GOT PROBLEMS!
CHK-CHACK!
PEW!
PEW!
YOUR SARCASM ISN'T HELPING THINGS.
OMNITRIX DON'T FAIL ME NOW!
NO CHICKENS!

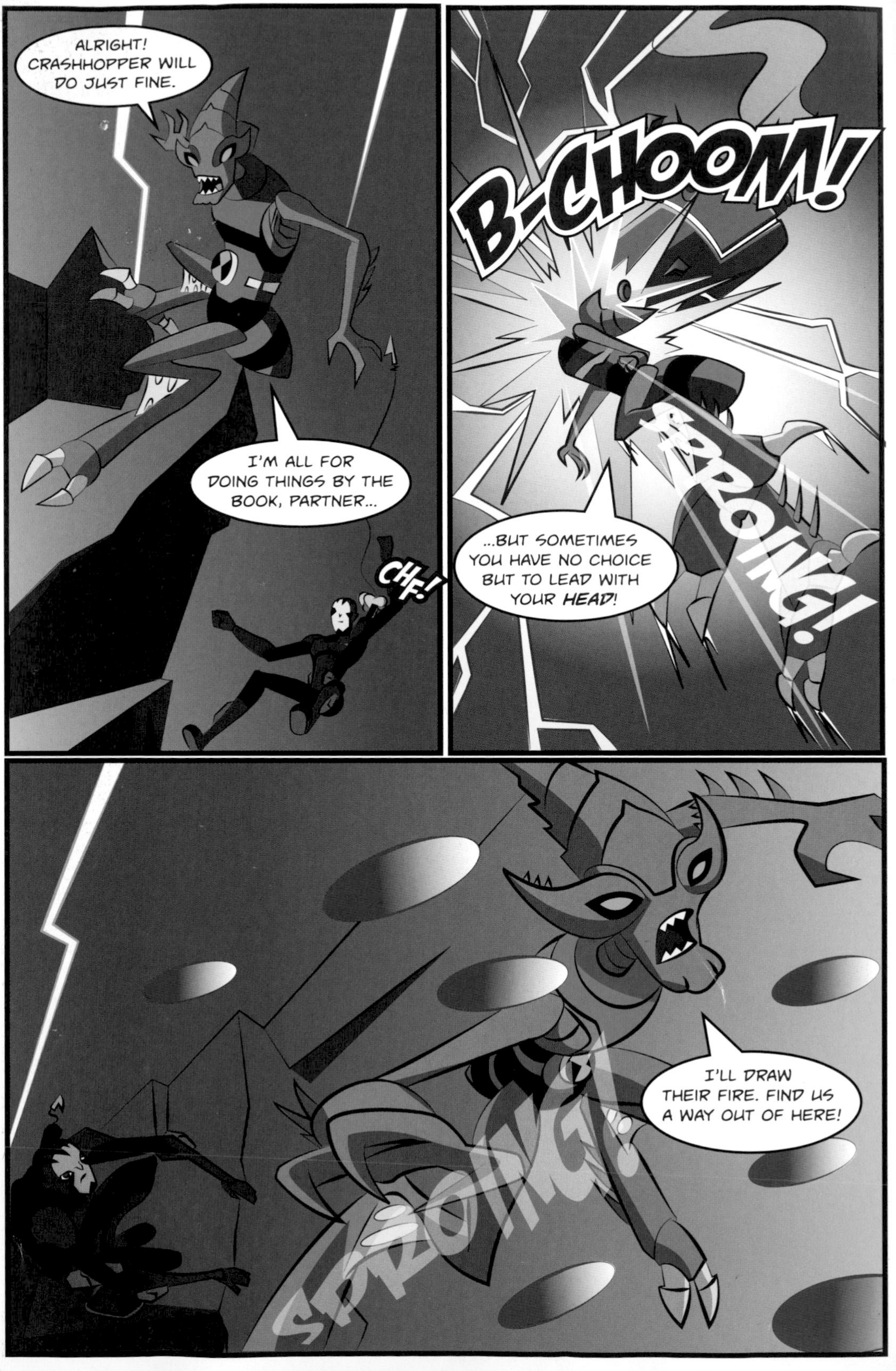
ALRIGHT! CRASHHOPPER WILL DO JUST FINE.
I'M ALL FOR DOING THINGS BY THE BOOK, PARTNER...
CHF!
B-CHOOM!
SPROING!
...BUT SOMETIMES YOU HAVE NO CHOICE BUT TO LEAD WITH YOUR **HEAD**!
I'LL DRAW THEIR FIRE. FIND US A WAY OUT OF HERE!
SPROING!

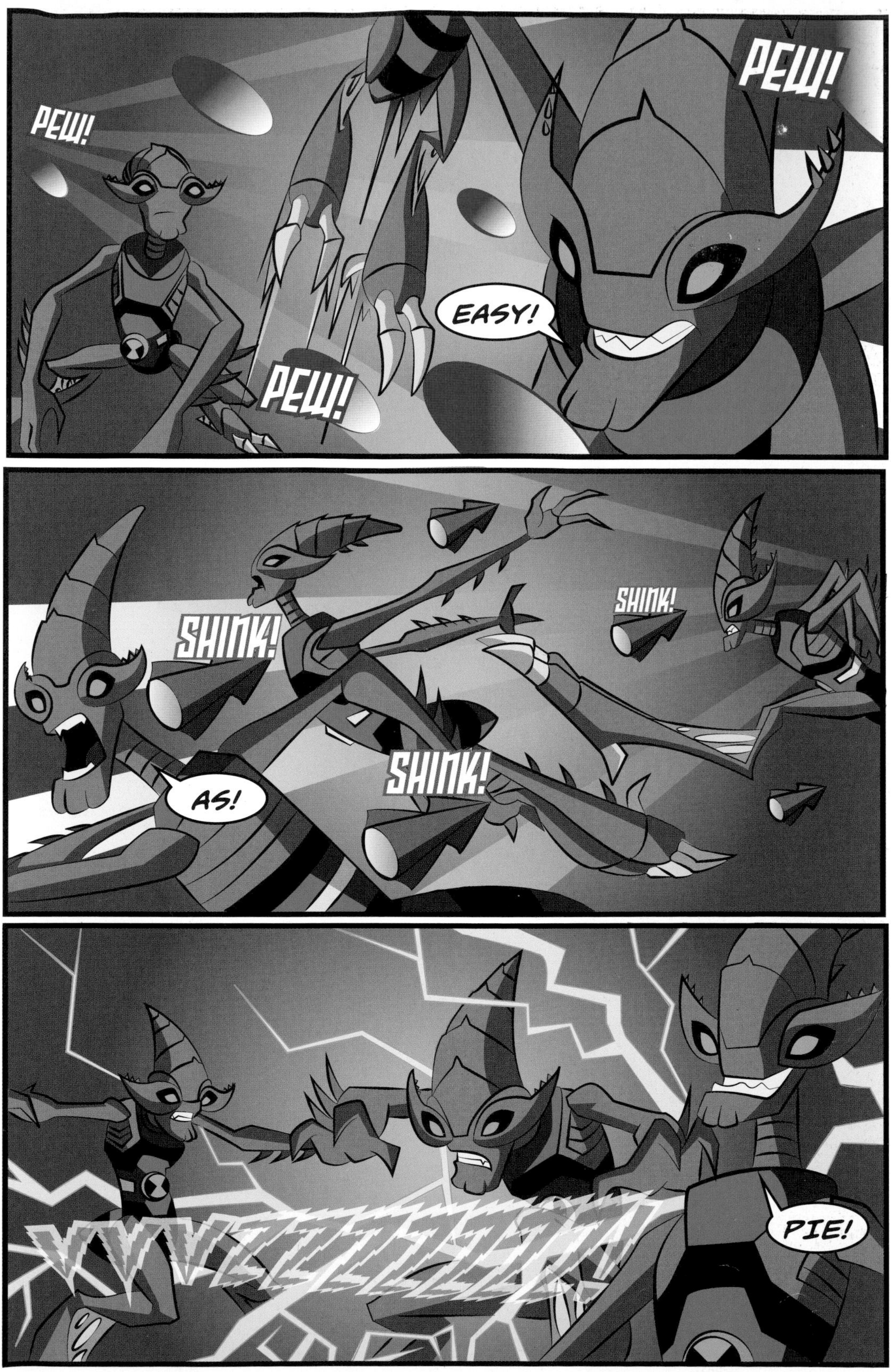
PEW!
PEW!
EASY!
PEW!
SHINK!
SHINK!
AS!
SHINK!
PIE!

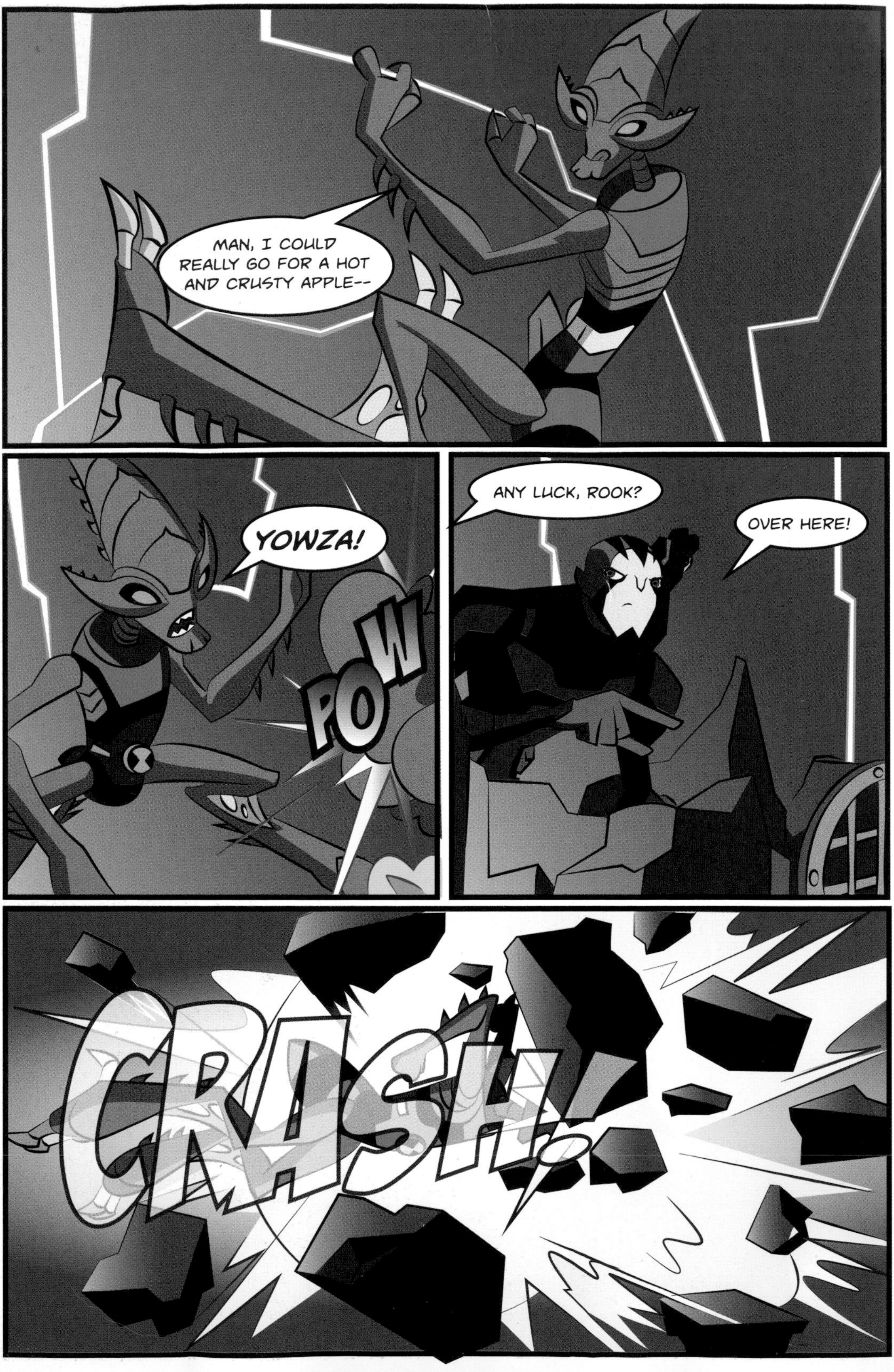
MAN, I COULD REALLY GO FOR A HOT AND CRUSTY APPLE--
YOWZA!
POW
ANY LUCK, ROOK?
OVER HERE!
CRASH!

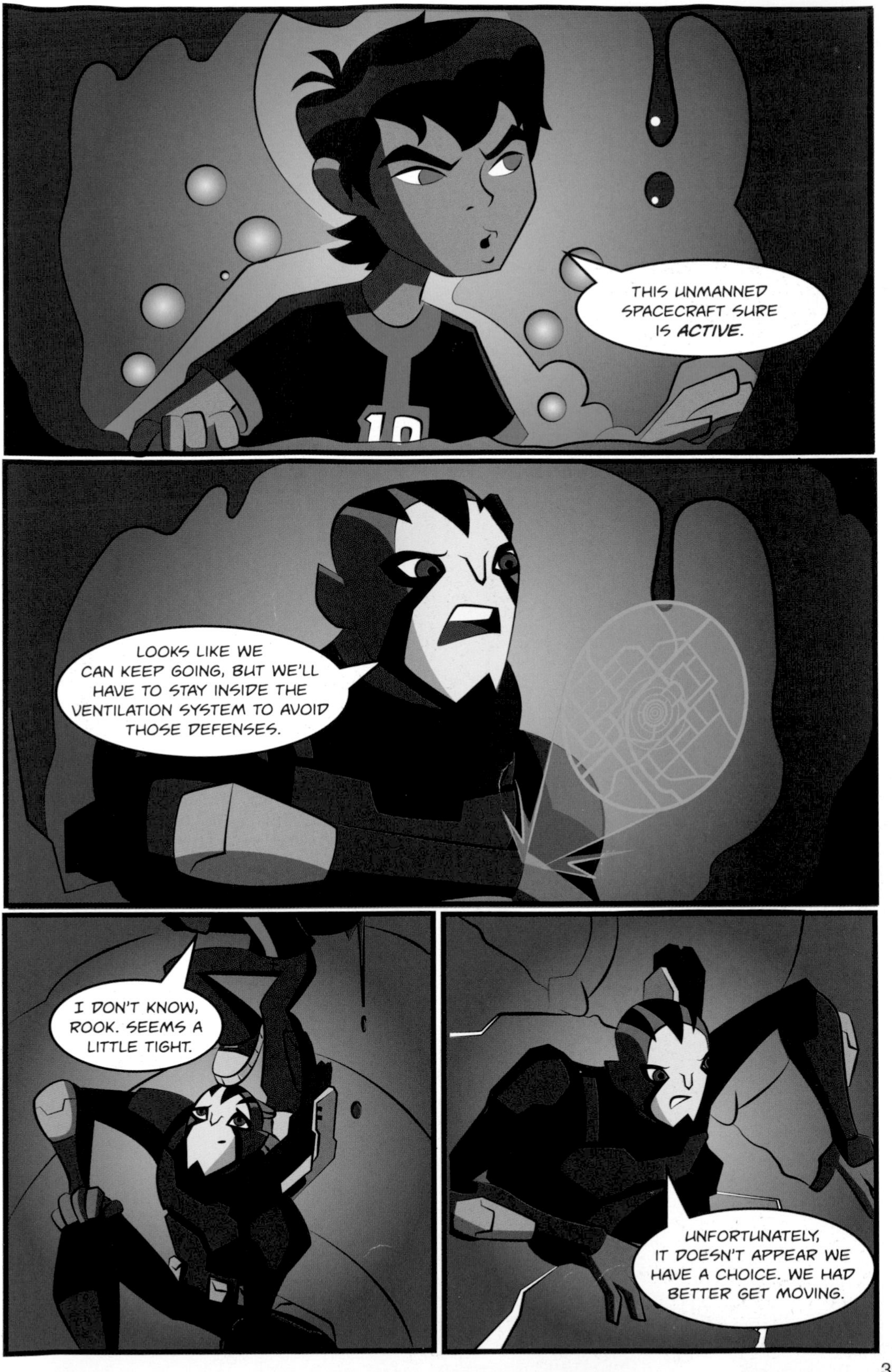
THIS UNMANNED SPACECRAFT SURE IS ACTIVE.
LOOKS LIKE WE CAN KEEP GOING, BUT WE'LL HAVE TO STAY INSIDE THE VENTILATION SYSTEM TO AVOID THOSE DEFENSES.
I DON'T KNOW, ROOK. SEEMS A LITTLE TIGHT.
UNFORTUNATELY, IT DOESN'T APPEAR WE HAVE A CHOICE. WE HAD BETTER GET MOVING.

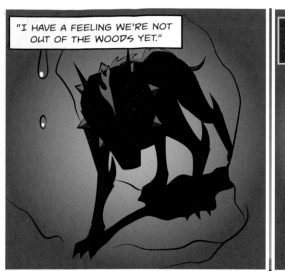

"I HAVE A FEELING WE'RE NOT OUT OF THE WOODS YET."

NOW IS THE TIME TO STRIKE! DO NOT DISAPPOINT ME, MY PET.

DO WHATEVER IT TAKES TO BRING BEN TENNYSON TO ME!

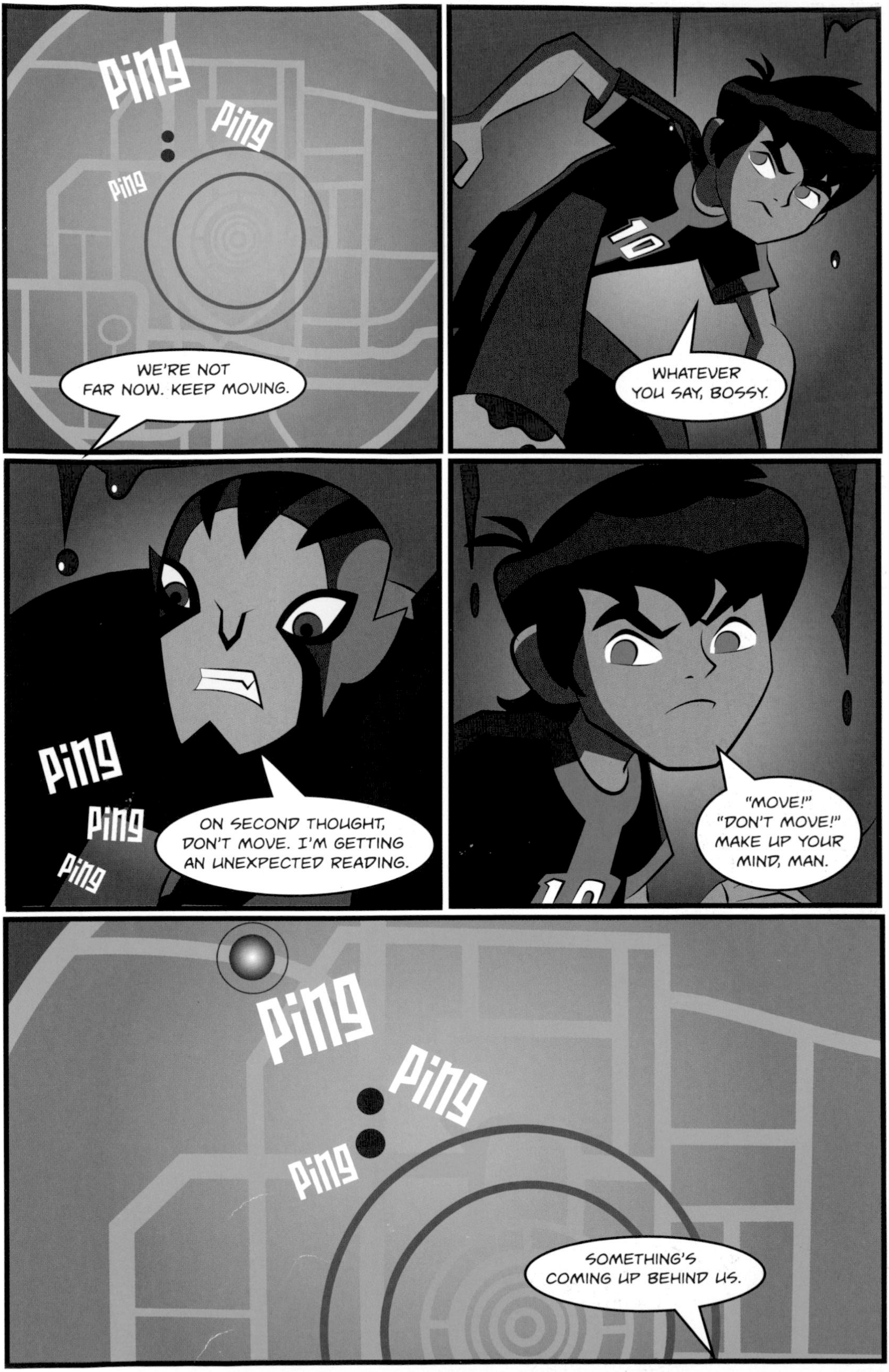
PING
PING
PING
WE'RE NOT FAR NOW. KEEP MOVING.
WHATEVER YOU SAY, BOSSY.
ON SECOND THOUGHT, DON'T MOVE. I'M GETTING AN UNEXPECTED READING.
PING
PING
PING
"MOVE!" "DON'T MOVE!" MAKE UP YOUR MIND, MAN.
PING
PING
PING
SOMETHING'S COMING UP BEHIND US.

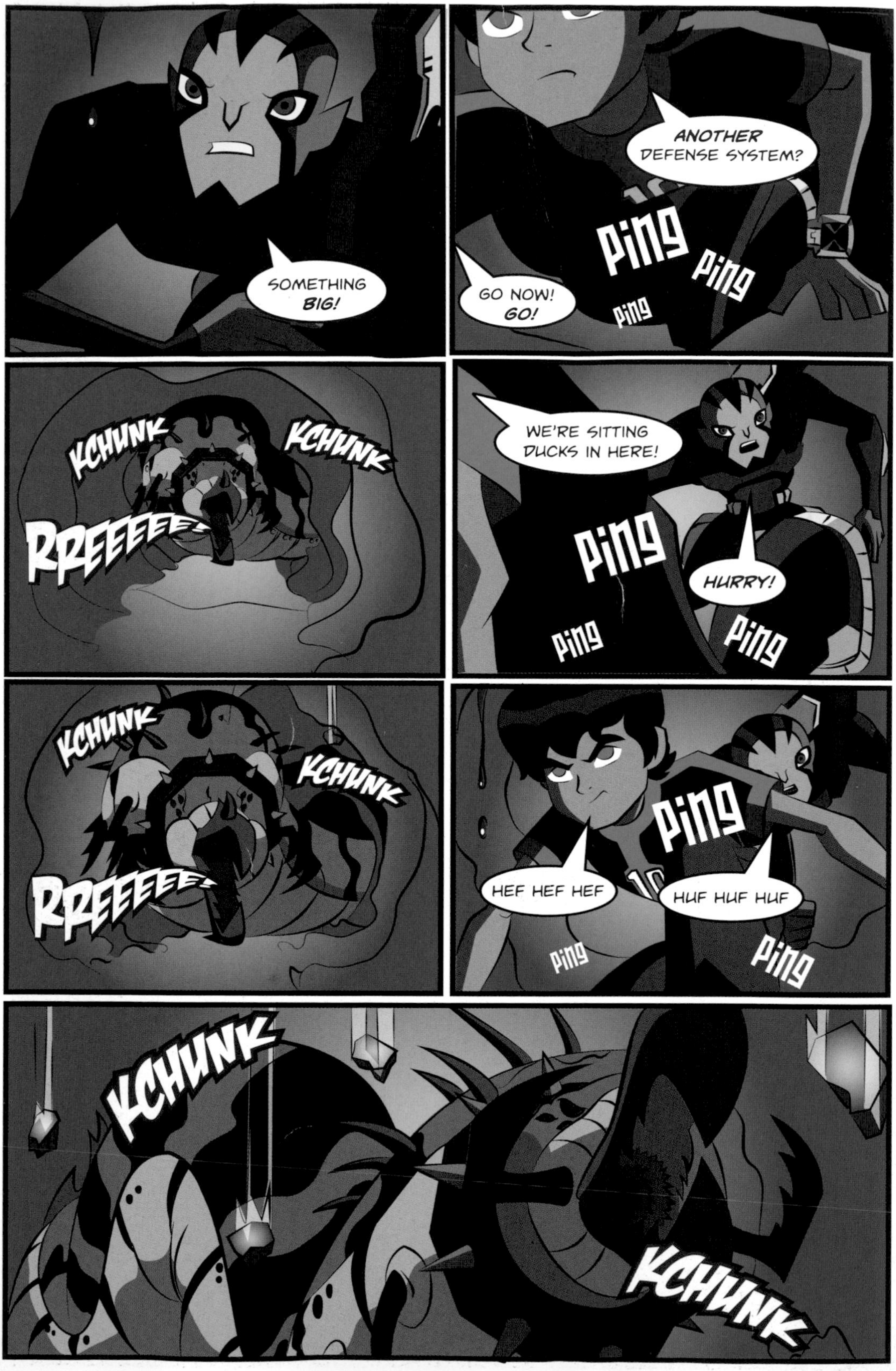
SOMETHING BIG!
ANOTHER DEFENSE SYSTEM?
PING PING PING
GO NOW! GO!
KCHUNK KCHUNK
RREEEEEE!
WE'RE SITTING DUCKS IN HERE!
PING
HURRY!
PING PING
KCHUNK KCHUNK
RREEEEEE!
PING
HEF HEF HEF
HUF HUF HUF
PING PING
KCHUNK
KCHUNK

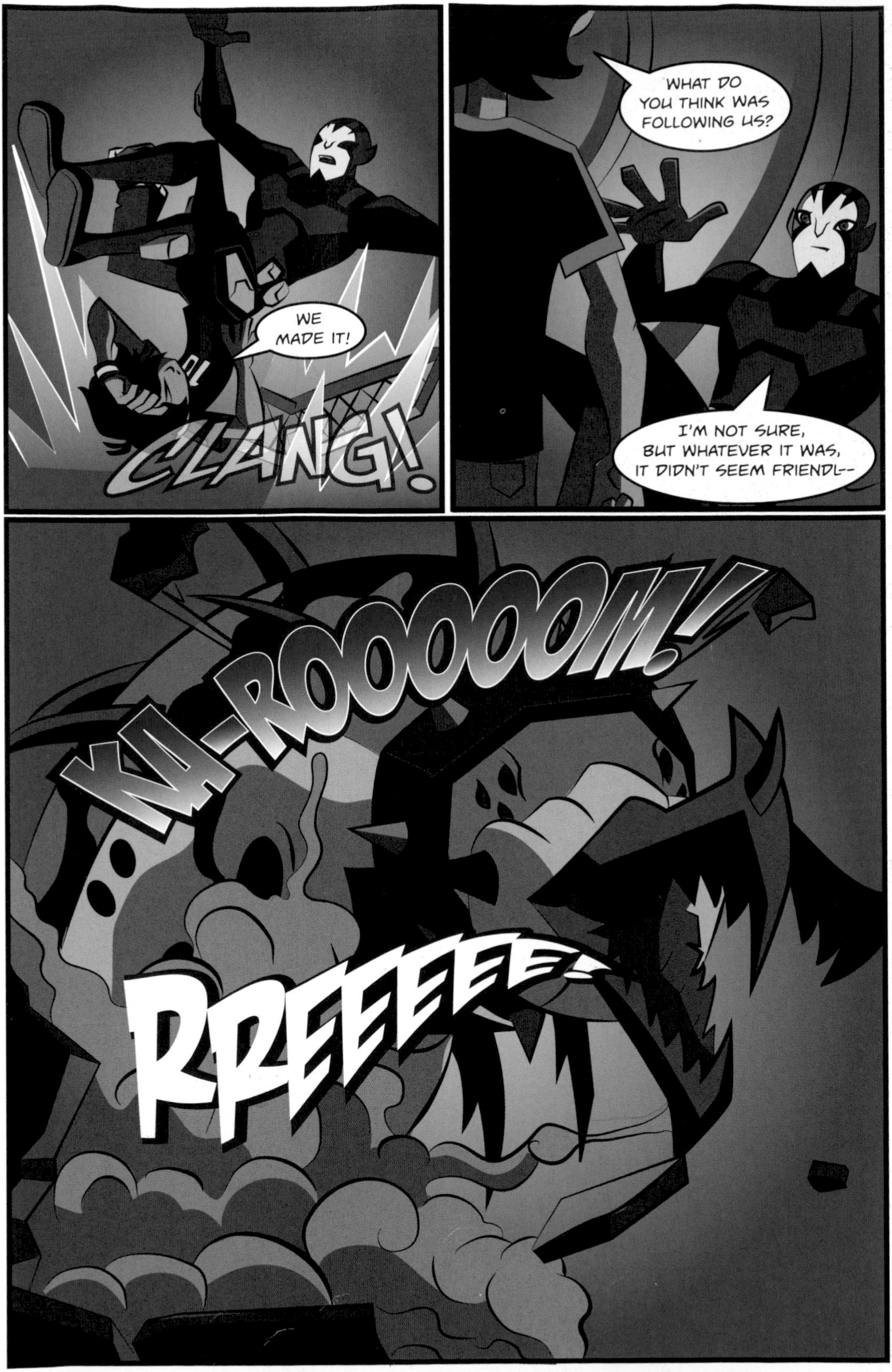
WE MADE IT!
CLANG!
WHAT DO YOU THINK WAS FOLLOWING US?
I'M NOT SURE, BUT WHATEVER IT WAS, IT DIDN'T SEEM FRIENDL--
KA-ROOOOOM!
RREEEEEE

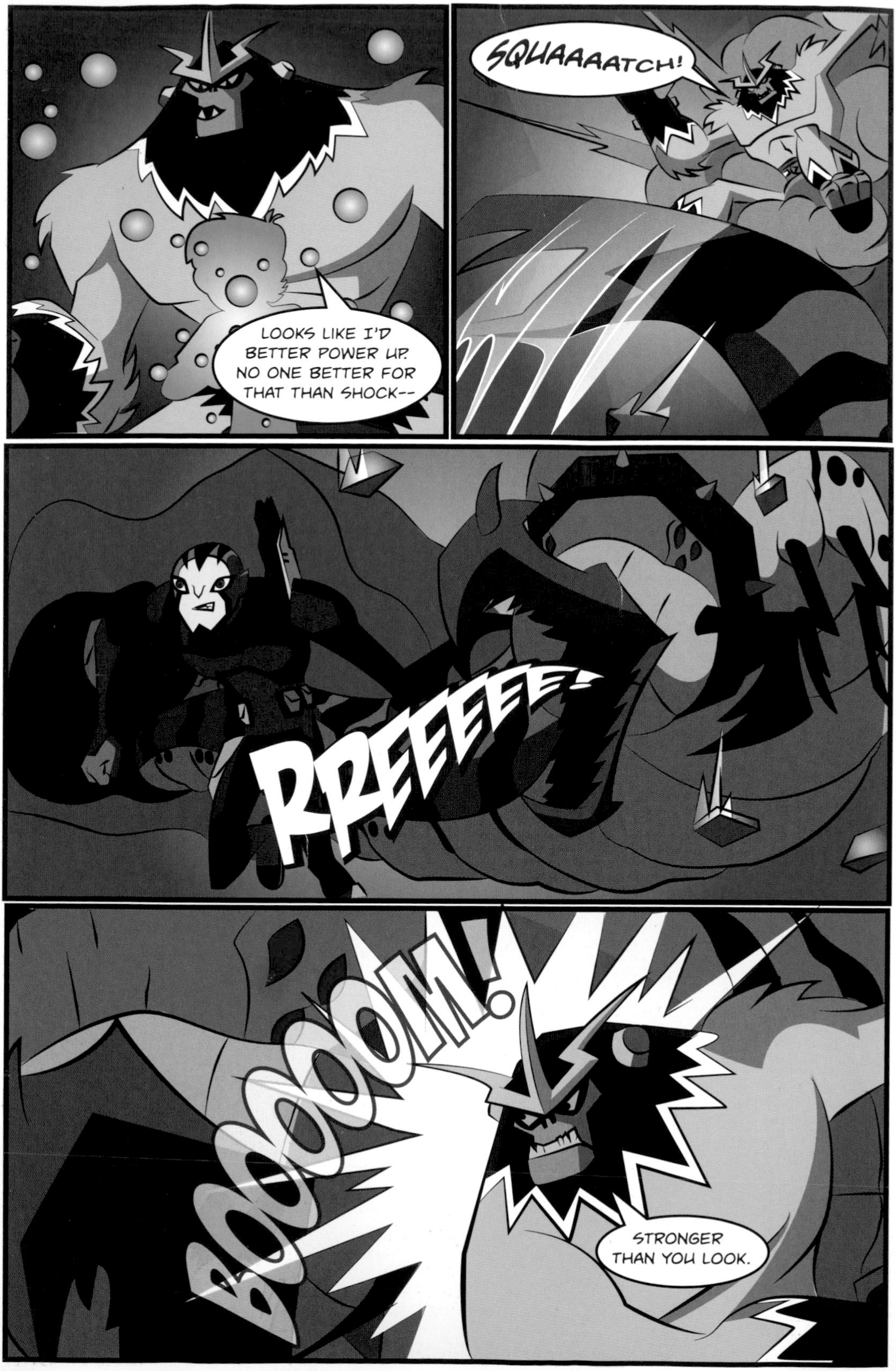
LOOKS LIKE I'D BETTER POWER UP. NO ONE BETTER FOR THAT THAN SHOCK--
SQUAAAAATCH!
RREEEEEE!
BOOOOOOM!
STRONGER THAN YOU LOOK.

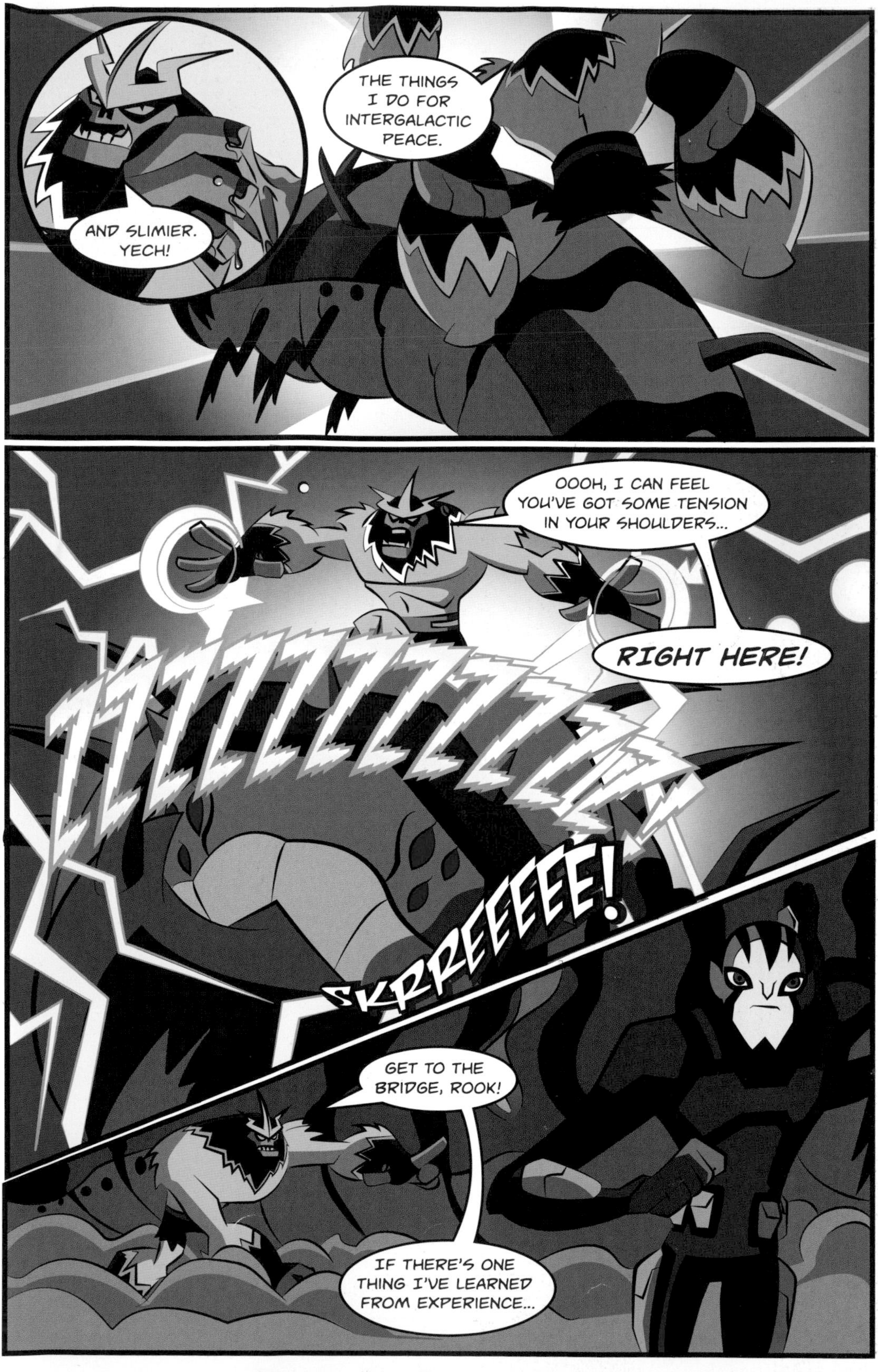
THE THINGS I DO FOR INTERGALACTIC PEACE.
AND SLIMIER. YECH!
OOOH, I CAN FEEL YOU'VE GOT SOME TENSION IN YOUR SHOULDERS...
RIGHT HERE!
ZZZZZZZZZZZAP!
SKRREEEEEE!
GET TO THE BRIDGE, ROOK!
IF THERE'S ONE THING I'VE LEARNED FROM EXPERIENCE...

...IT'S THAT THE BIG GUYS DON'T STAY DOWN VERY LONG!

COME ON, BEN. *RUN!*

WHAT DOES IT LOOK LIKE I'M DOING?!

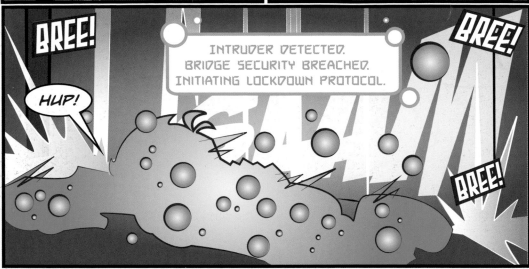

BREE!

BREE!

BREE!

HUP!

INTRUDER DETECTED. BRIDGE SECURITY BREACHED. INITIATING LOCKDOWN PROTOCOL.

THOOOM!

HEY ROOK, I THINK WE FOUND WHAT YOU WERE LOOKING FOR...

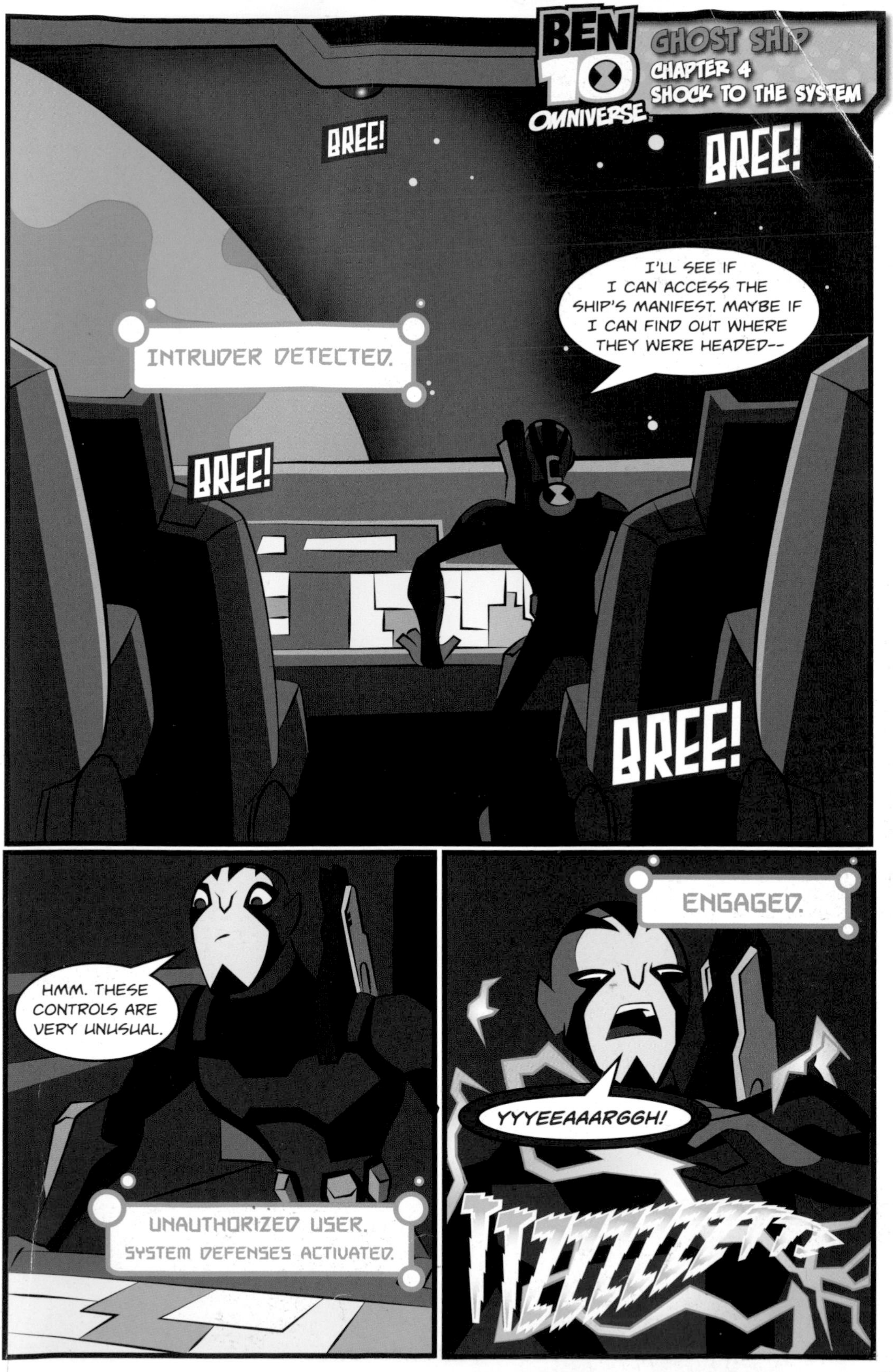
BEN 10 OMNIVERSE
GHOST SHIP
CHAPTER 4
SHOCK TO THE SYSTEM
BREE!
BREE!
INTRUDER DETECTED.
I'LL SEE IF I CAN ACCESS THE SHIP'S MANIFEST. MAYBE IF I CAN FIND OUT WHERE THEY WERE HEADED--
BREE!
BREE!
HMM. THESE CONTROLS ARE VERY UNUSUAL.
UNAUTHORIZED USER. SYSTEM DEFENSES ACTIVATED.
ENGAGED.
YYYEEAAARGGH!

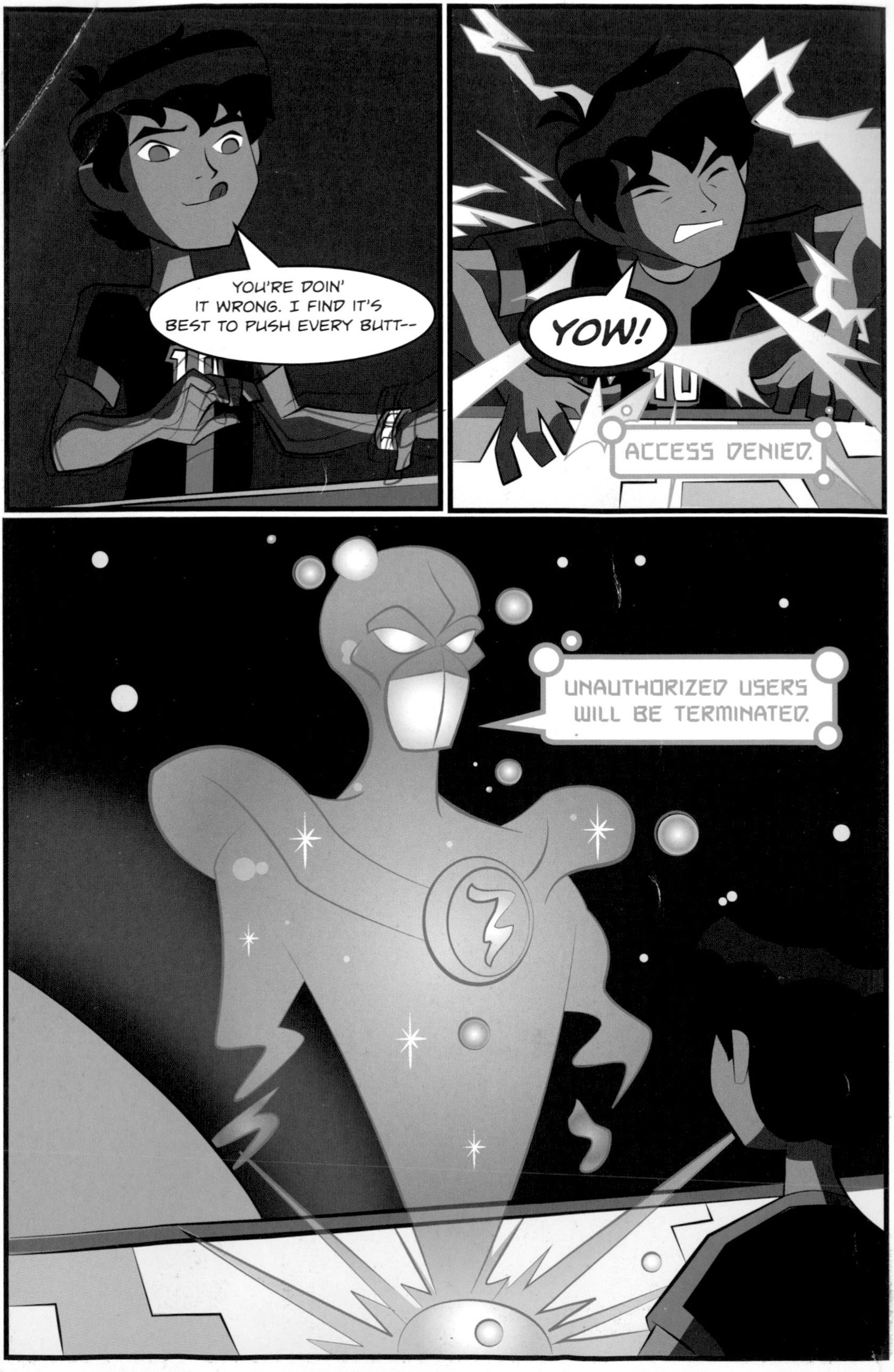
YOU'RE DOIN' IT WRONG. I FIND IT'S BEST TO PUSH EVERY BUTT--
YOW!
ACCESS DENIED.
UNAUTHORIZED USERS WILL BE TERMINATED.

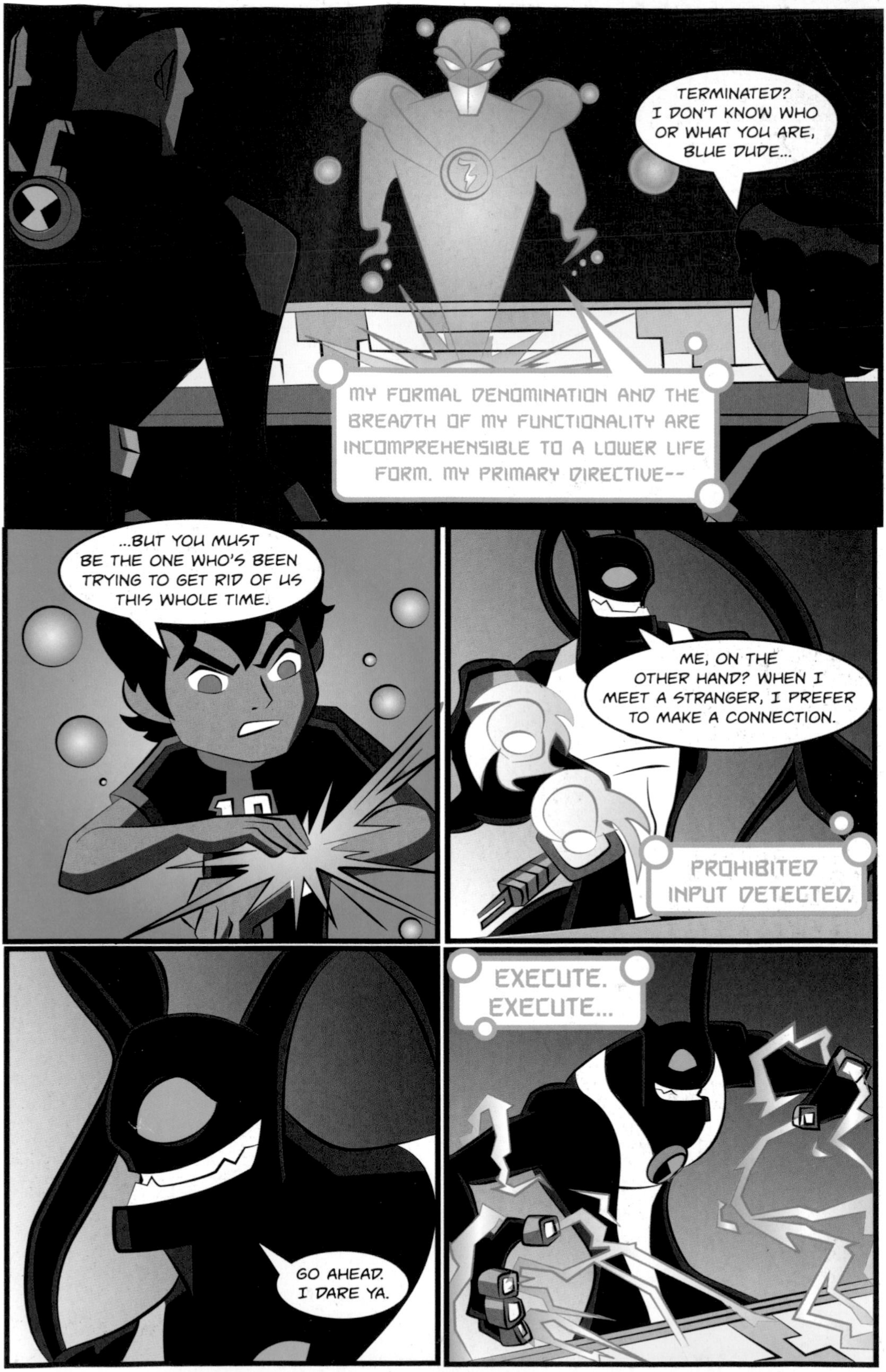
TERMINATED? I DON'T KNOW WHO OR WHAT YOU ARE, BLUE DUDE...
MY FORMAL DENOMINATION AND THE BREADTH OF MY FUNCTIONALITY ARE INCOMPREHENSIBLE TO A LOWER LIFE FORM. MY PRIMARY DIRECTIVE--
...BUT YOU MUST BE THE ONE WHO'S BEEN TRYING TO GET RID OF US THIS WHOLE TIME.
ME, ON THE OTHER HAND? WHEN I MEET A STRANGER, I PREFER TO MAKE A CONNECTION.
PROHIBITED INPUT DETECTED.
GO AHEAD. I DARE YA.
EXECUTE. EXECUTE...

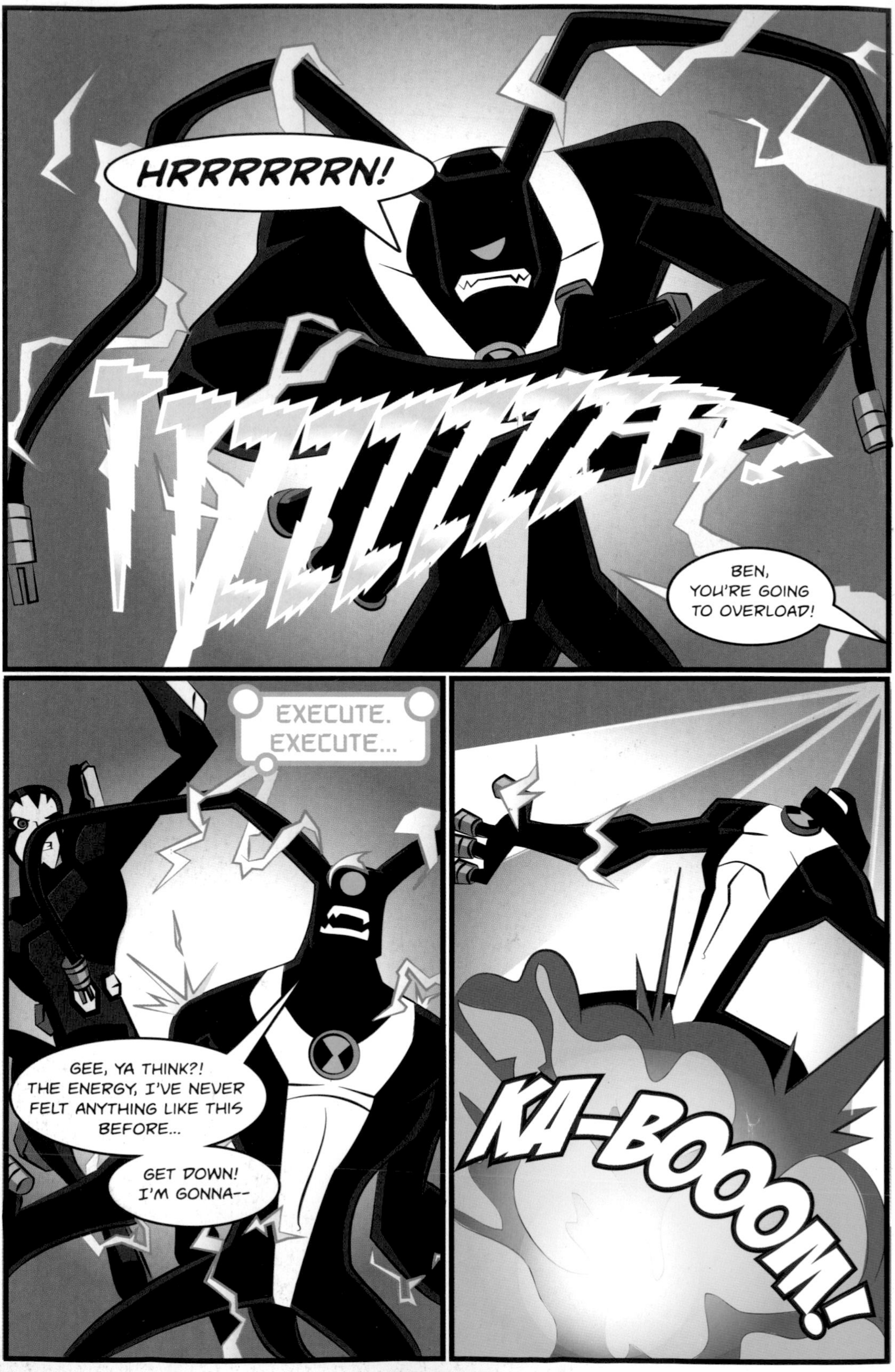
HRRRRRRN!
BEN, YOU'RE GOING TO OVERLOAD!
EXECUTE. EXECUTE...
GEE, YA THINK?! THE ENERGY, I'VE NEVER FELT ANYTHING LIKE THIS BEFORE...
GET DOWN! I'M GONNA--
KA-BOOOOM!

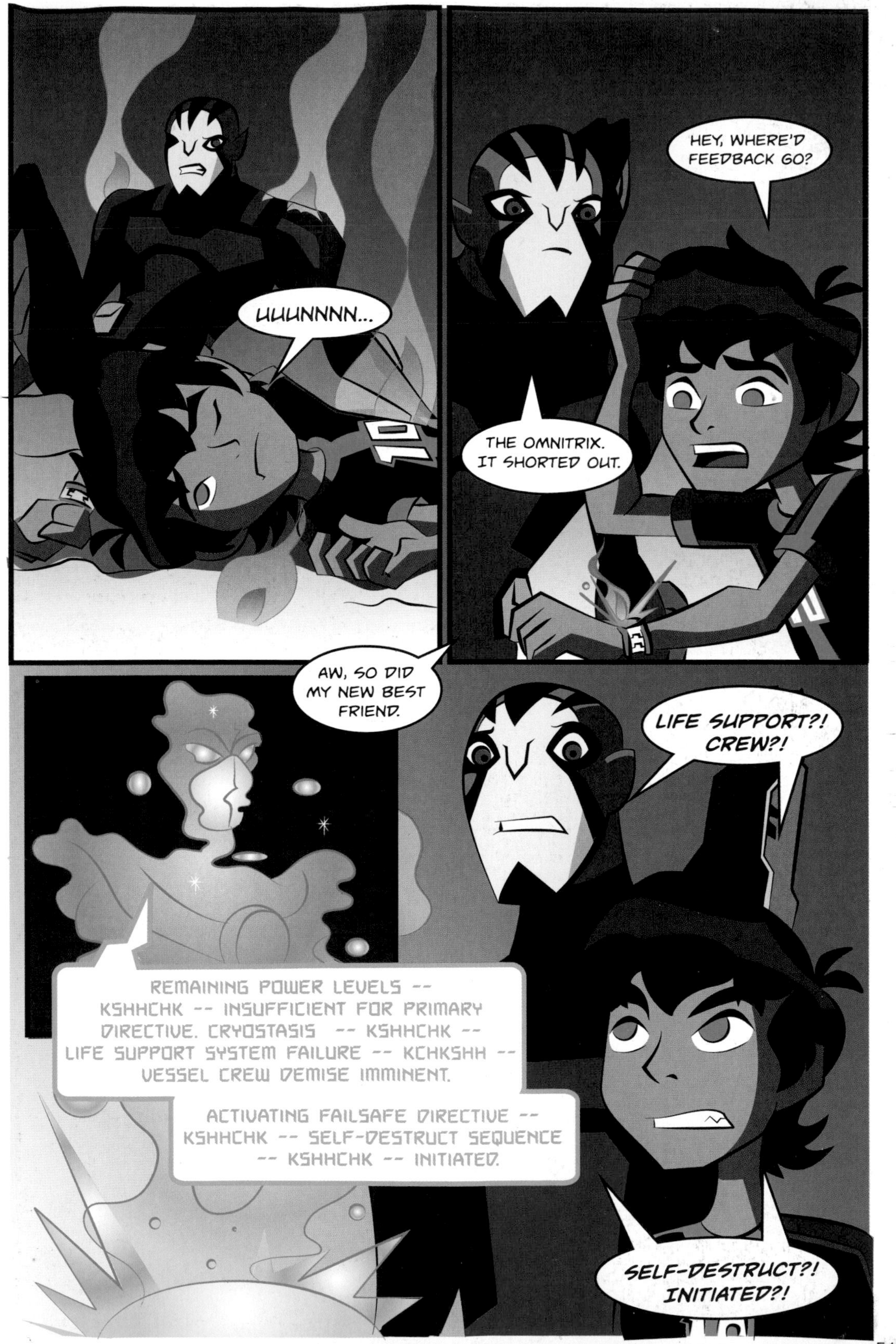
UUUNNNN...
HEY, WHERE'D FEEDBACK GO?
THE OMNITRIX. IT SHORTED OUT.
AW, SO DID MY NEW BEST FRIEND.
REMAINING POWER LEVELS -- KSHHCHK -- INSUFFICIENT FOR PRIMARY DIRECTIVE. CRYOSTASIS -- KSHHCHK -- LIFE SUPPORT SYSTEM FAILURE -- KCHKSHH -- VESSEL CREW DEMISE IMMINENT.
ACTIVATING FAILSAFE DIRECTIVE -- KSHHCHK -- SELF-DESTRUCT SEQUENCE -- KSHHCHK -- INITIATED.
LIFE SUPPORT?! CREW?!
SELF-DESTRUCT?! INITIATED?!

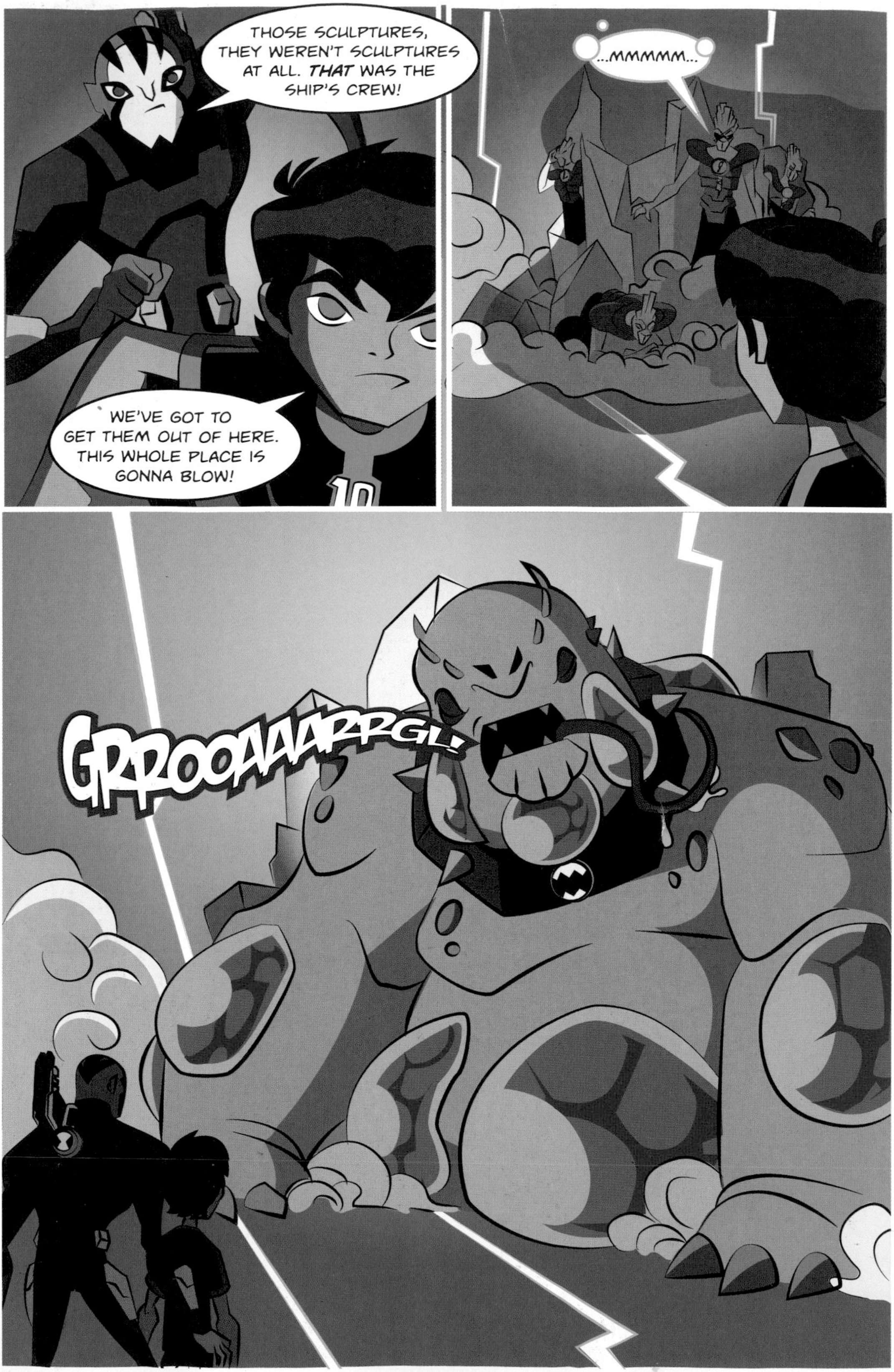
THOSE SCULPTURES, THEY WEREN'T SCULPTURES AT ALL. *THAT* WAS THE SHIP'S CREW!
WE'VE GOT TO GET THEM OUT OF HERE. THIS WHOLE PLACE IS GONNA BLOW!
...MMMMM...
GRROOAAARRGL!

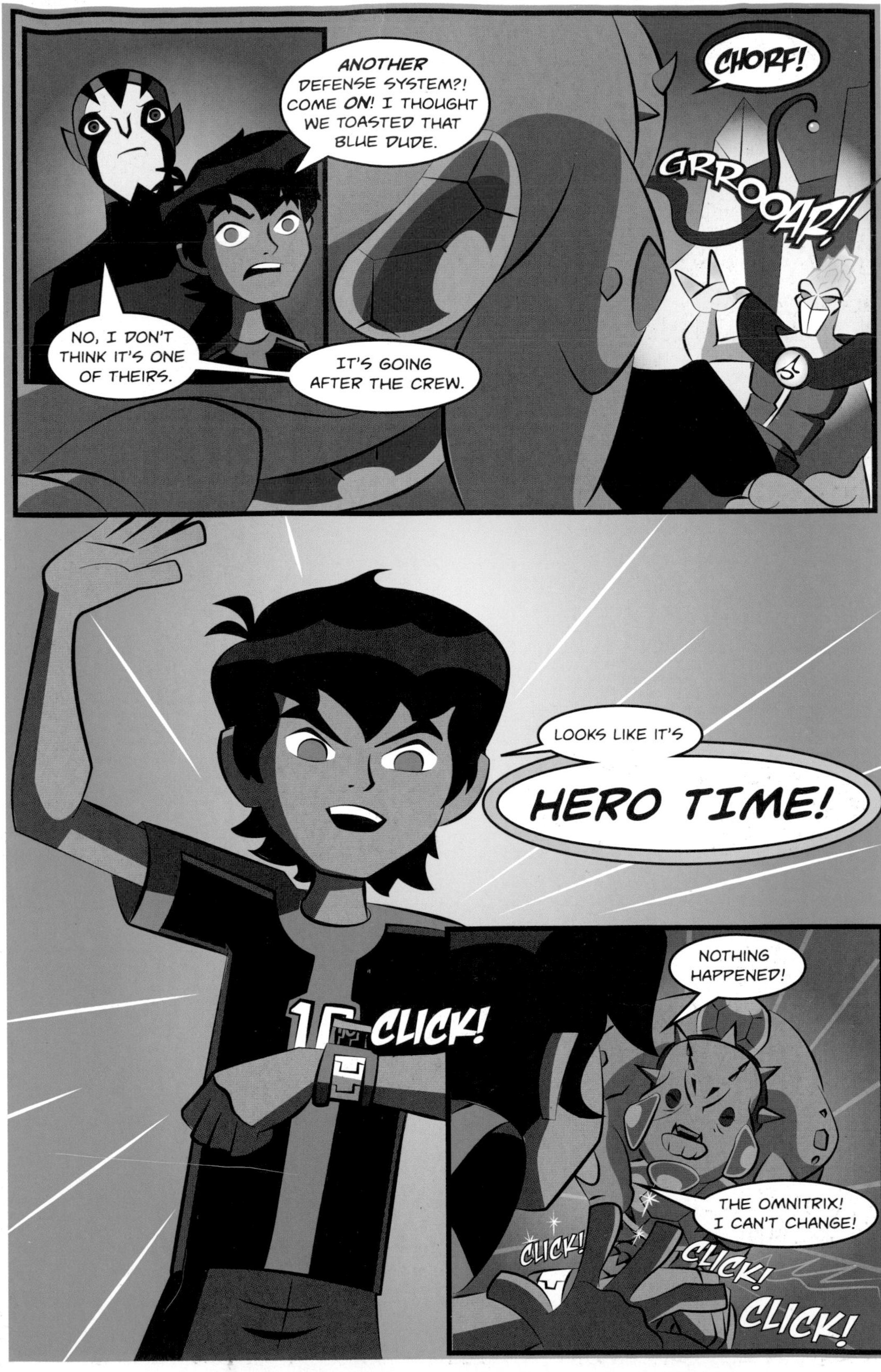
ANOTHER DEFENSE SYSTEM?! COME ON! I THOUGHT WE TOASTED THAT BLUE DUDE.
CHORF!
GRRROOAR!
NO, I DON'T THINK IT'S ONE OF THEIRS.
IT'S GOING AFTER THE CREW.
LOOKS LIKE IT'S
HERO TIME!
CLICK!
NOTHING HAPPENED!
THE OMNITRIX! I CAN'T CHANGE!
CLICK!
CLICK!
CLICK!

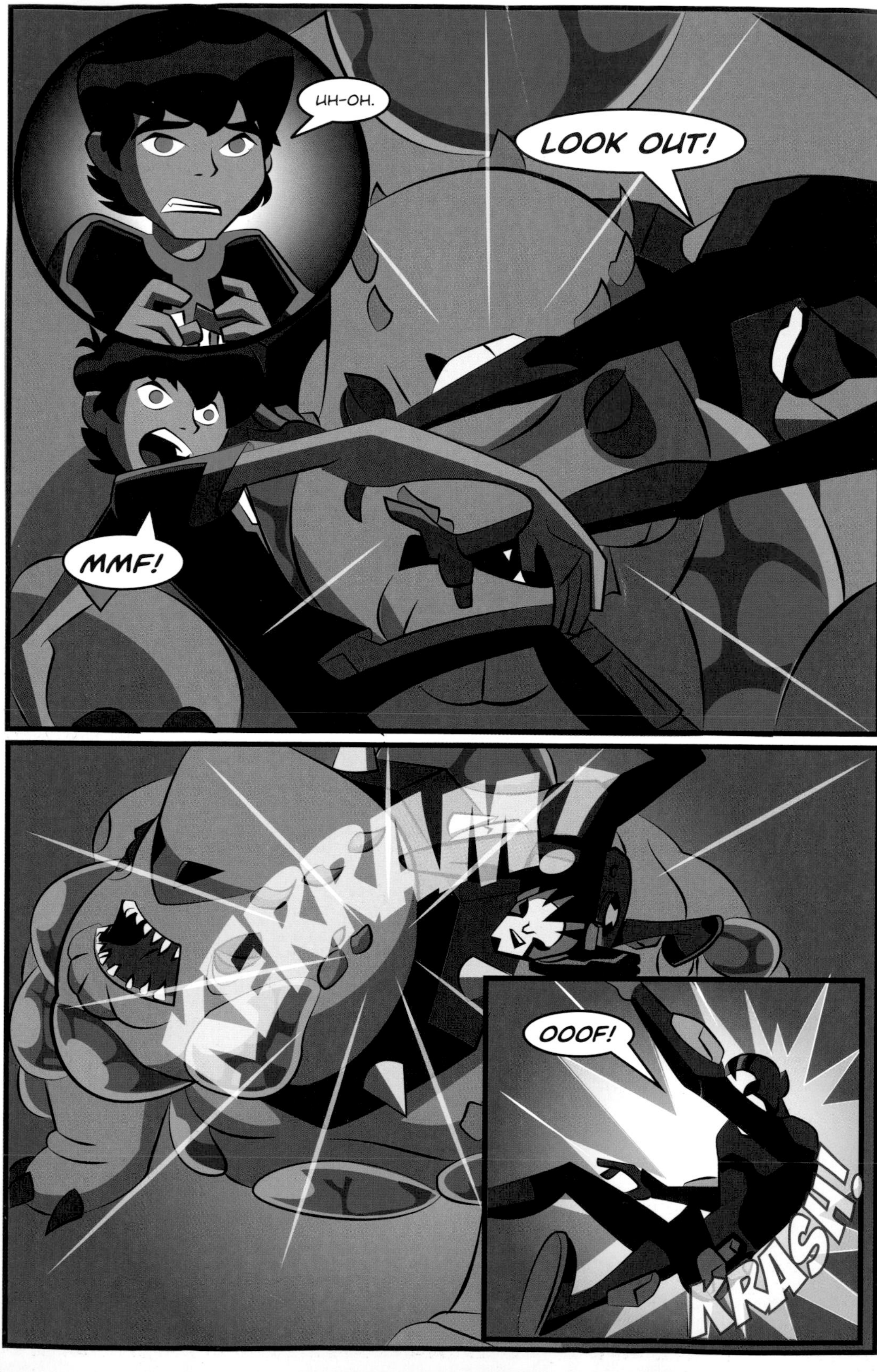
UH-OH.
LOOK OUT!
MMF!
OOOF!
KRASH!!

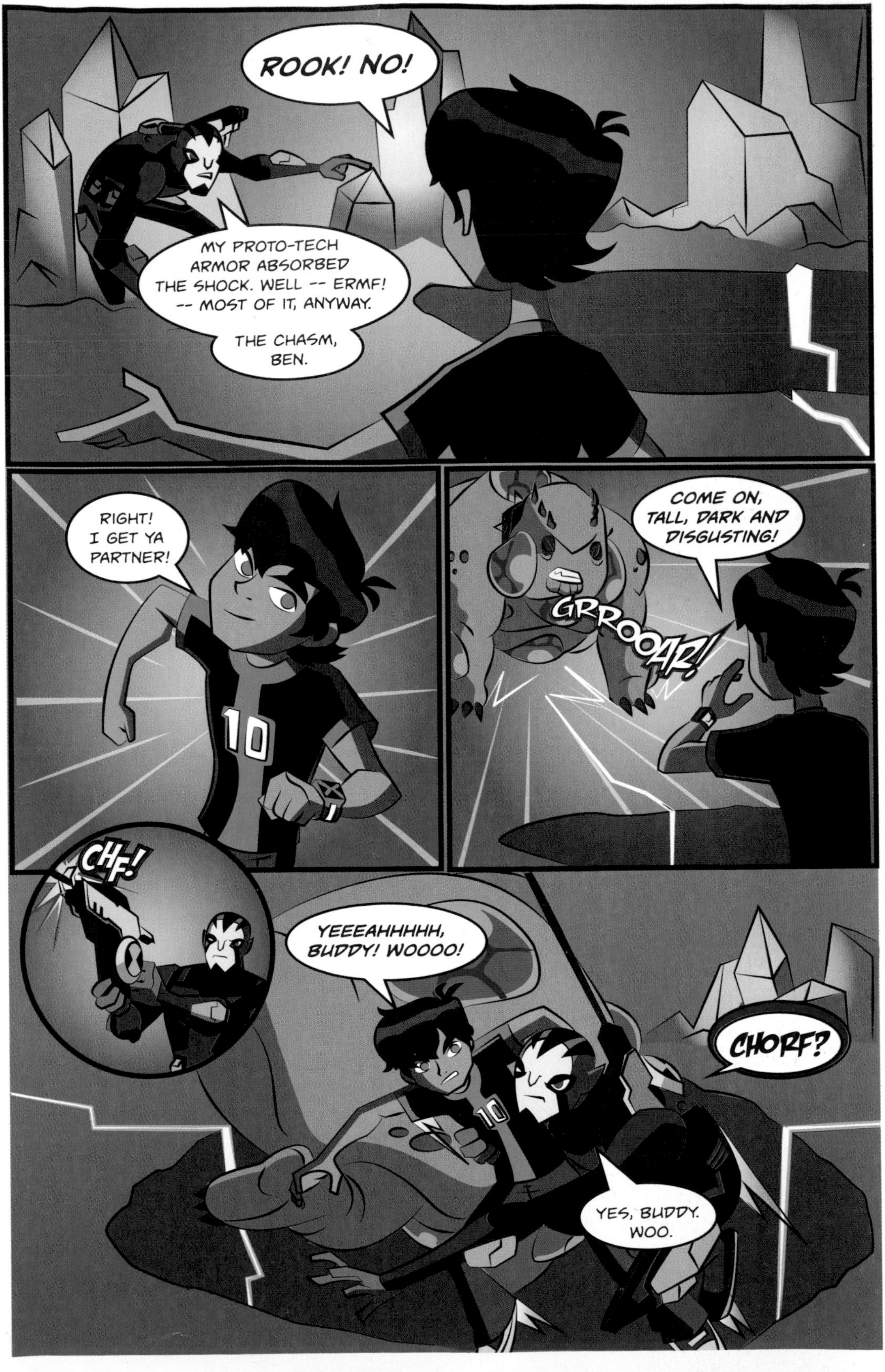
ROOK! NO!
MY PROTO-TECH ARMOR ABSORBED THE SHOCK. WELL -- ERMF! -- MOST OF IT, ANYWAY.
THE CHASM, BEN.
RIGHT! I GET YA PARTNER!
COME ON, TALL, DARK AND DISGUSTING!
GRROOOAR!
CHF!
YEEEAHHHHH, BUDDY! WOOOO!
CHORF?
YES, BUDDY. WOO.

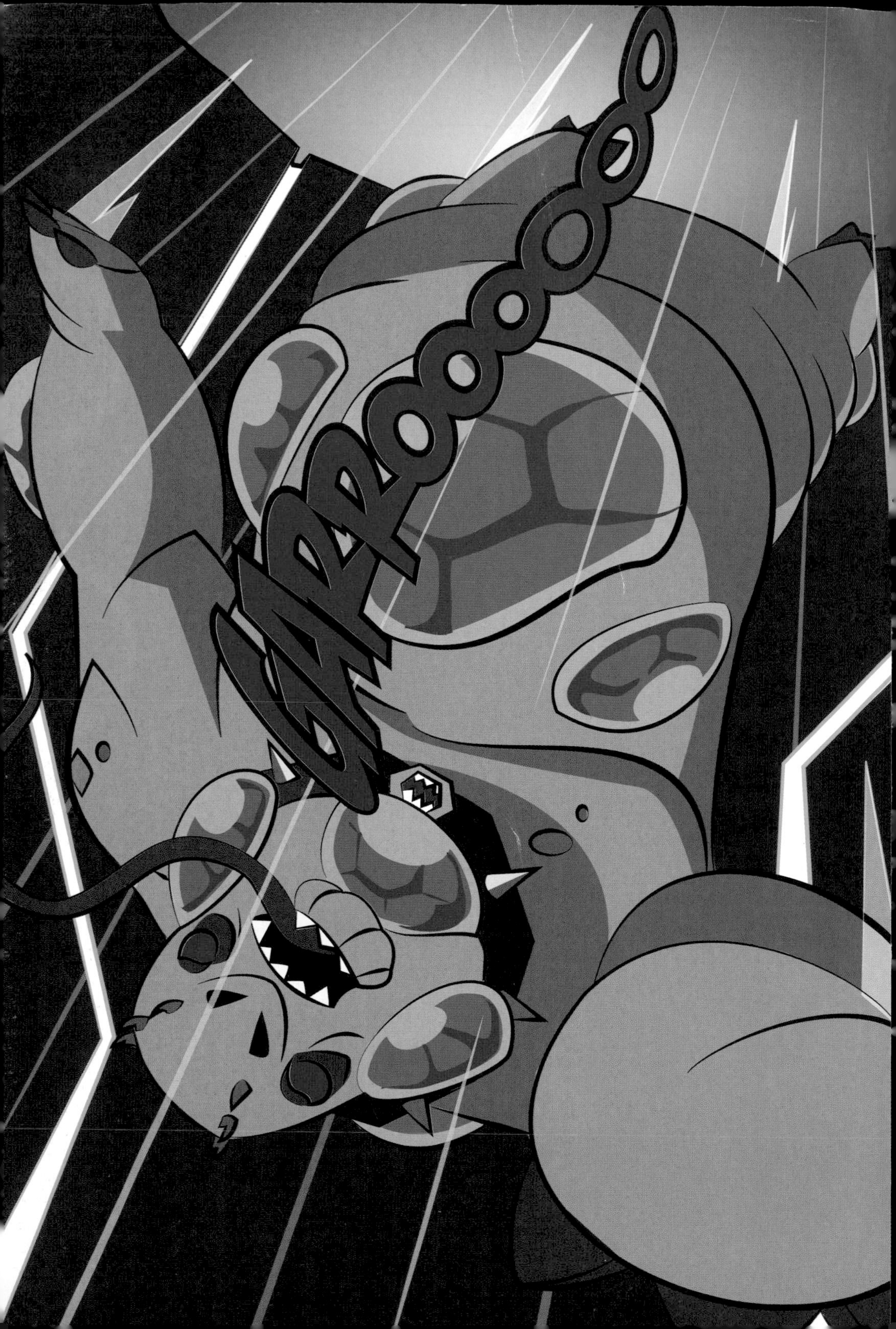
GARROOOOOOO

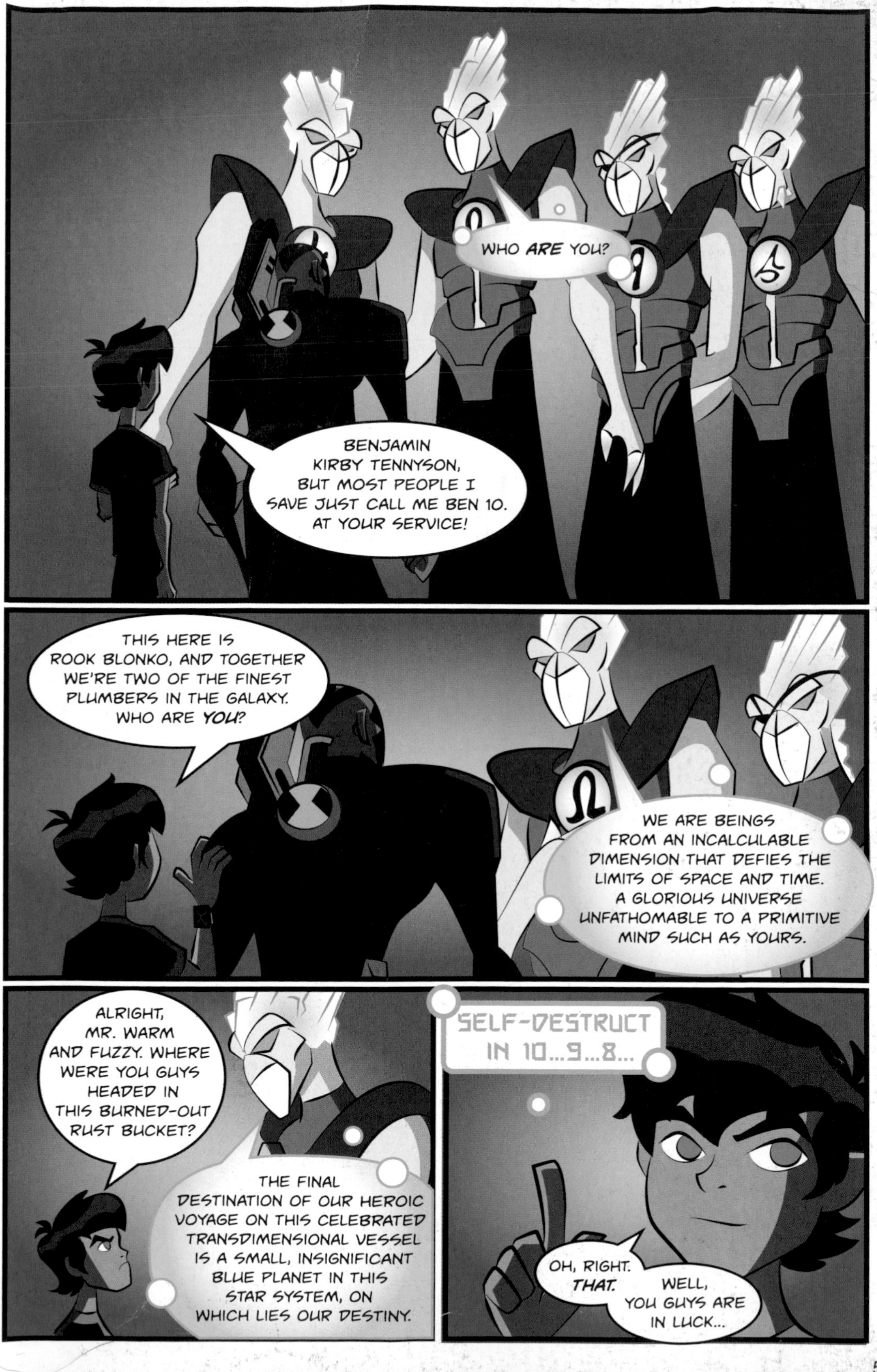
WHO ARE YOU?
BENJAMIN KIRBY TENNYSON, BUT MOST PEOPLE I SAVE JUST CALL ME BEN 10. AT YOUR SERVICE!
THIS HERE IS ROOK BLONKO, AND TOGETHER WE'RE TWO OF THE FINEST PLUMBERS IN THE GALAXY. WHO ARE YOU?
WE ARE BEINGS FROM AN INCALCULABLE DIMENSION THAT DEFIES THE LIMITS OF SPACE AND TIME. A GLORIOUS UNIVERSE UNFATHOMABLE TO A PRIMITIVE MIND SUCH AS YOURS.
ALRIGHT, MR. WARM AND FUZZY. WHERE WERE YOU GUYS HEADED IN THIS BURNED-OUT RUST BUCKET?
THE FINAL DESTINATION OF OUR HEROIC VOYAGE ON THIS CELEBRATED TRANSDIMENSIONAL VESSEL IS A SMALL, INSIGNIFICANT BLUE PLANET IN THIS STAR SYSTEM, ON WHICH LIES OUR DESTINY.
SELF-DESTRUCT IN 10...9...8...
OH, RIGHT. THAT.
WELL, YOU GUYS ARE IN LUCK...

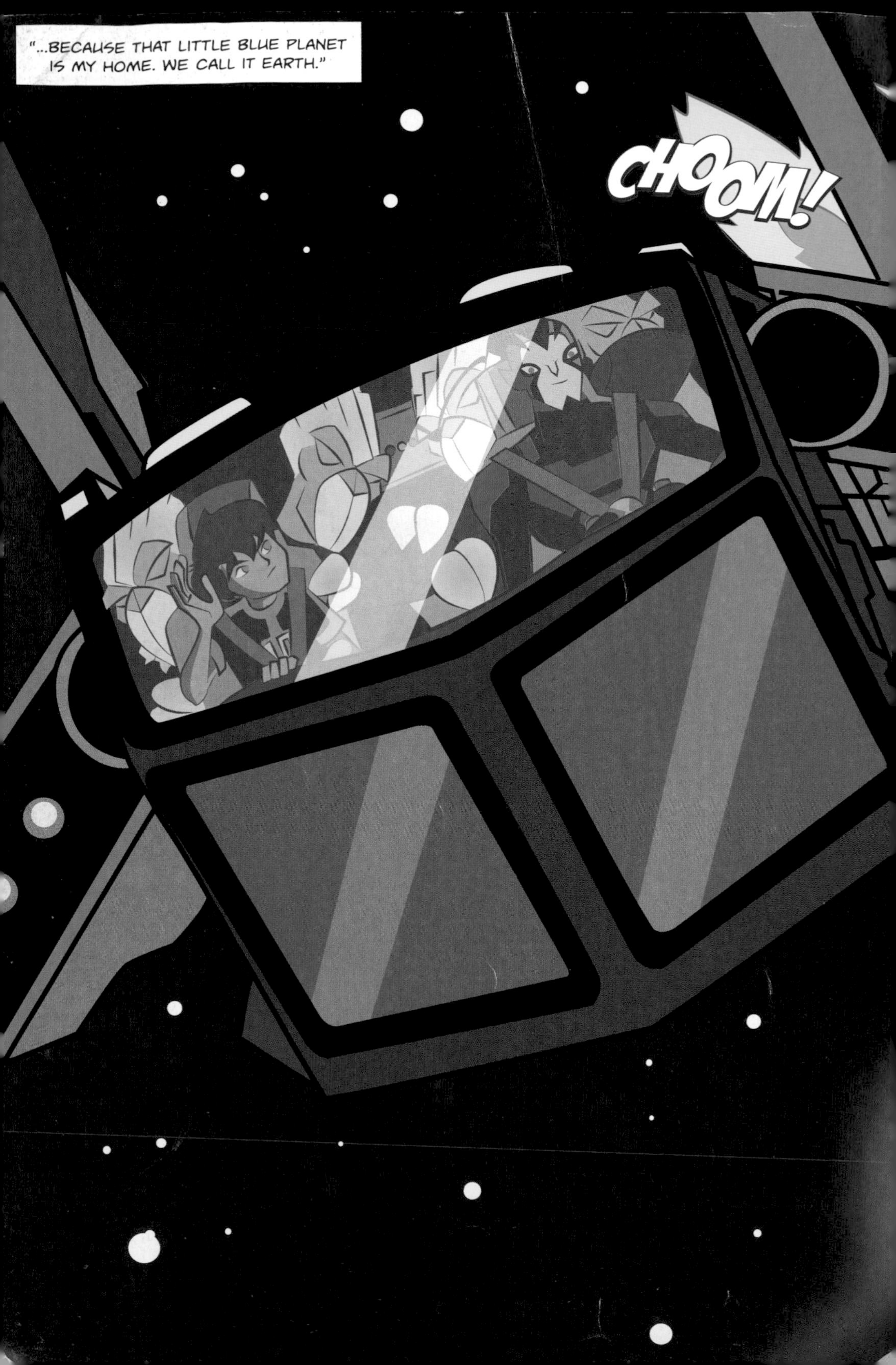
"...BECAUSE THAT LITTLE BLUE PLANET IS MY HOME. WE CALL IT EARTH."
CHOOM!

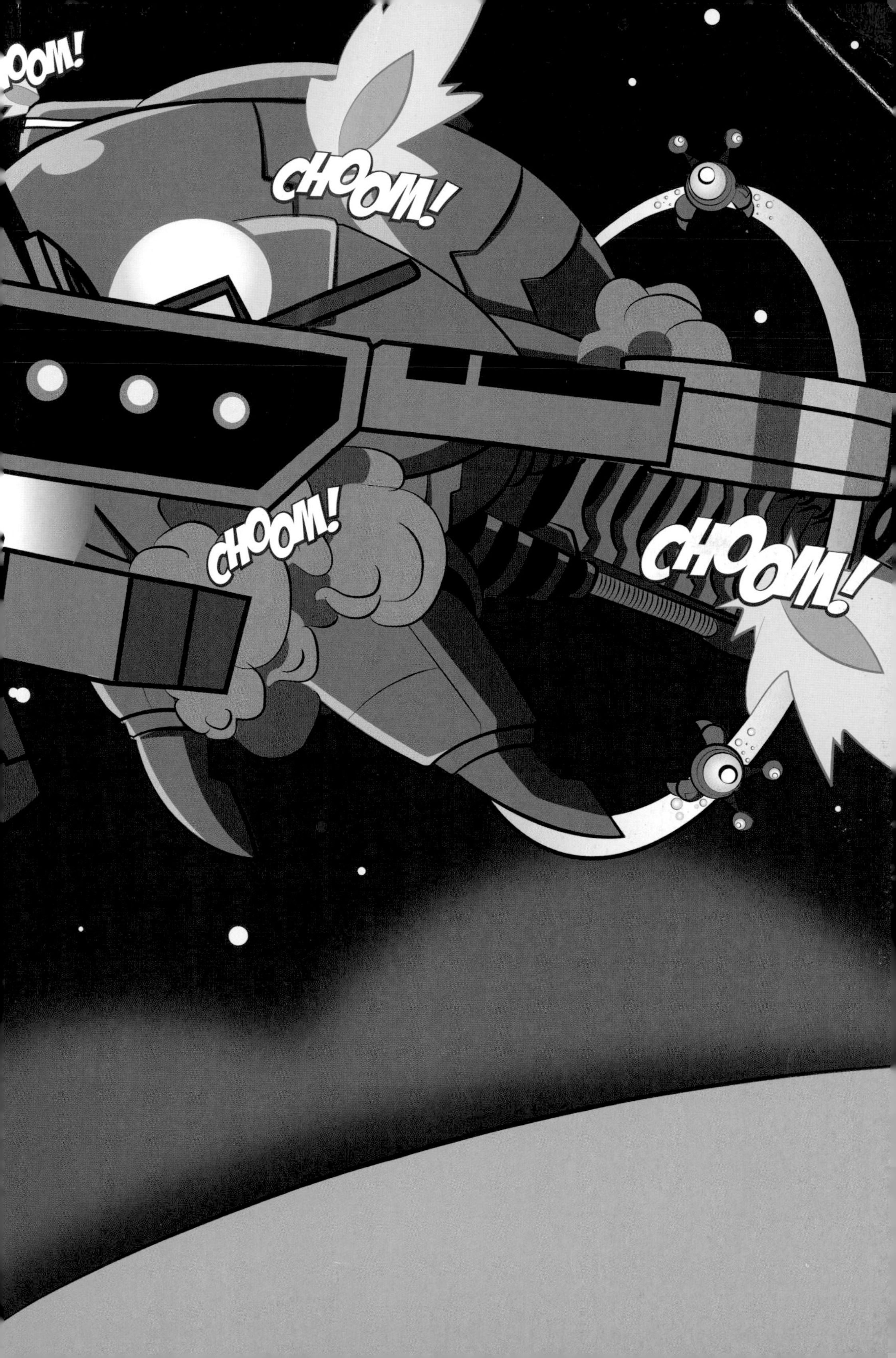
OOM!
CHOOM!
CHOOM!
CHOOM!

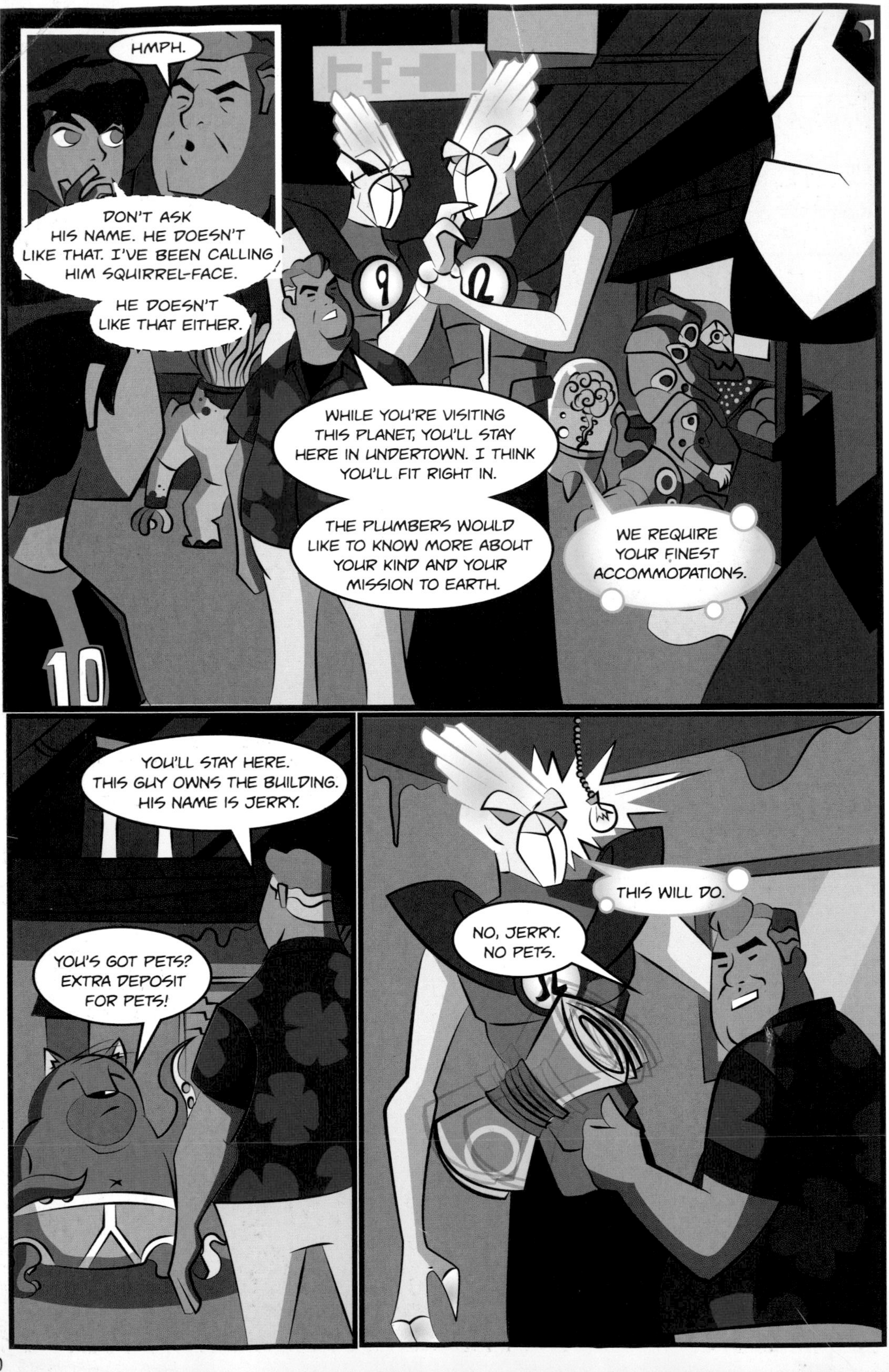
HMPH.
DON'T ASK HIS NAME. HE DOESN'T LIKE THAT. I'VE BEEN CALLING HIM SQUIRREL-FACE.
HE DOESN'T LIKE THAT EITHER.
WHILE YOU'RE VISITING THIS PLANET, YOU'LL STAY HERE IN UNDERTOWN. I THINK YOU'LL FIT RIGHT IN.
THE PLUMBERS WOULD LIKE TO KNOW MORE ABOUT YOUR KIND AND YOUR MISSION TO EARTH.
WE REQUIRE YOUR FINEST ACCOMMODATIONS.
YOU'LL STAY HERE. THIS GUY OWNS THE BUILDING. HIS NAME IS JERRY.
YOU'S GOT PETS? EXTRA DEPOSIT FOR PETS!
THIS WILL DO.
NO, JERRY. NO PETS.

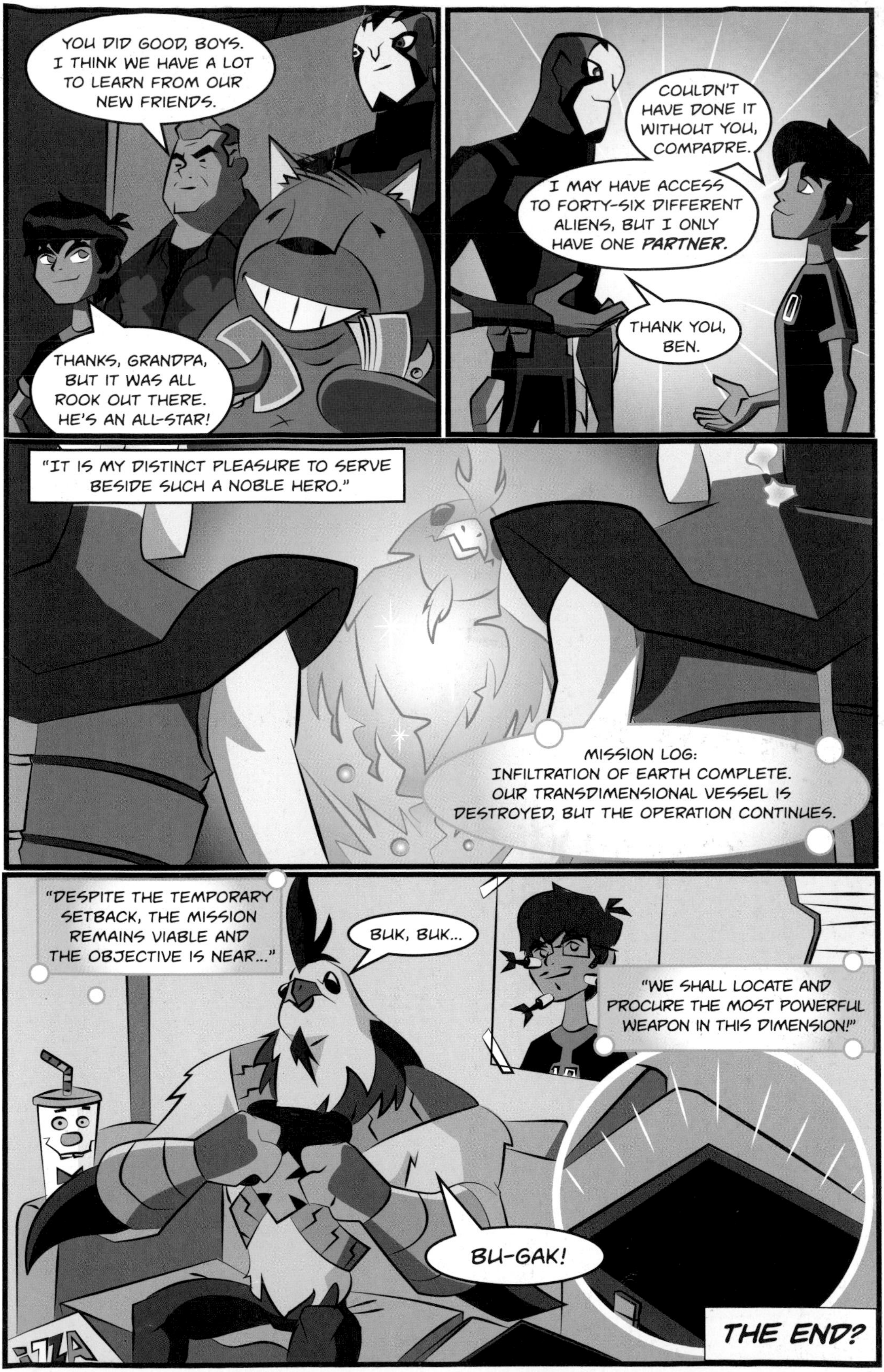
YOU DID GOOD, BOYS. I THINK WE HAVE A LOT TO LEARN FROM OUR NEW FRIENDS.
THANKS, GRANDPA, BUT IT WAS ALL ROOK OUT THERE. HE'S AN ALL-STAR!
COULDN'T HAVE DONE IT WITHOUT YOU, COMPADRE.
I MAY HAVE ACCESS TO FORTY-SIX DIFFERENT ALIENS, BUT I ONLY HAVE ONE PARTNER.
THANK YOU, BEN.
"IT IS MY DISTINCT PLEASURE TO SERVE BESIDE SUCH A NOBLE HERO."
MISSION LOG: INFILTRATION OF EARTH COMPLETE. OUR TRANSDIMENSIONAL VESSEL IS DESTROYED, BUT THE OPERATION CONTINUES.
"DESPITE THE TEMPORARY SETBACK, THE MISSION REMAINS VIABLE AND THE OBJECTIVE IS NEAR..."
BUK, BUK...
"WE SHALL LOCATE AND PROCURE THE MOST POWERFUL WEAPON IN THIS DIMENSION!"
BU-GAK!
THE END?

BONUS SKETCH!

WRITER

CORY LEVINE IS A FORMER EDITORIAL STAFFER FOR MARVEL COMICS WHERE HE EDITED HUNDREDS OF COLLECTED EDITIONS OF COMIC BOOKS, ENCYCLOPEDIC HANDBOOKS, SPECIAL EDITION MAGAZINES AND FOREIGN-LICENSED COMICS INCLUDING THE COMPANY'S WELL-RECEIVED LINE OF *SOLEIL* GRAPHIC ALBUM ADAPTATIONS. HE WAS ALSO A WRITER ON *MONSUNO: REVENGE/SACRIFICE* (VOLUME 2) (VIZ MEDIA).

ARTIST

ALAN BROWN HAS WORKED AS A STORYBOARD AND CONCEPT ARTIST FOR A BUSY LONDON AGENCY, WORKING FOR CLIENTS SUCH AS LEGO AND FORD. AS A FREELANCE ARTIST AND DESIGNER HE HAS CREATED LICENSED ARTWORK FOR DISNEY, WARNER BROS. AND THE BBC, WHILE CONTINUING TO PROVIDE COMIC ART FOR SMALL PRESS AND INDEPENDENT COMICS.